D0445168

TOM ANGLEBERGER
& PAUL DELLINGER

FUZZY

AMULET BOOKS
NEW YORK

Cataloging-in-Publication Data has been applied for and may be obtained from the Library of Congress.

ISBN: 978-1-4197-2122-9
Text copyright © 2016 Tom Angleberger and Paul Dellinger
Book design by Chad W. Beckerman

Printed and bound in U.S.A.
10 9 8 7 6 5 4 3 2 1

Amulet Books are available at special discounts when purchased in quantity for premiums and promotions as well as fundraising or educational use. Special editions can also be created to specification. For details, contact specialsales@abramsbooks.com or the address below.

ABRAMS The Art of Books
115 West 18th Street, New York, NY 10011
abramsbooks.com

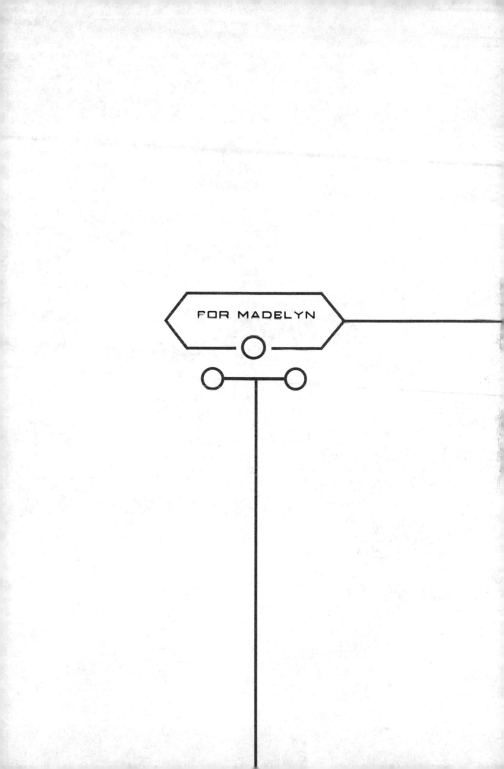

FOR MADELYN

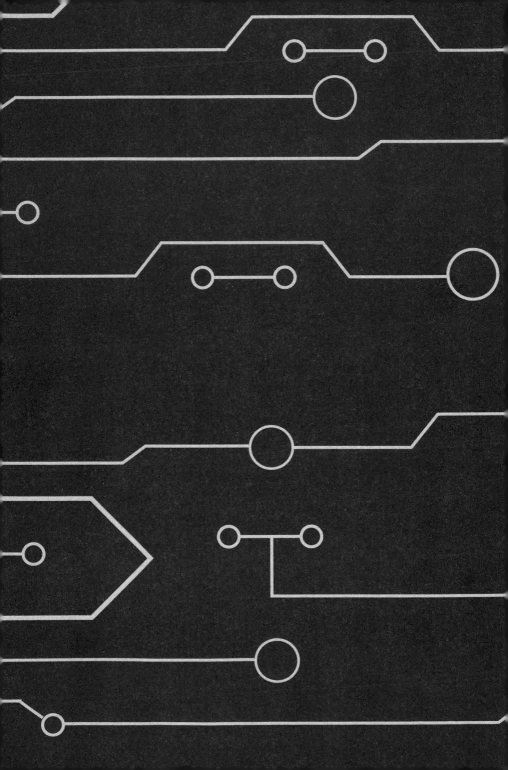

H, BIG WHOOP, MAXINE," SAID Krysti. "Another robot."

Max made a sound somewhere between a sigh and a growl.

First of all, Max didn't like being called Maxine, and Krysti knew it.

Second of all, Max *hated* the new trend of using fifty-year-old slang like "big whoop" and "awesome, bro," and Krysti knew it.

And most of all, Max *loved* robots, and Krysti knew that, too. So Krysti was pretending she wasn't interested in the biggest news of all time: Today was the day that the Robot Integration Program started. There had been a lot of hype about it and even some news coverage. Their school, Vanguard Middle, was getting the first-ever robot student. Anywhere. Ever. It *was* a big whoop, at least in Max's opinion.

Now Max was walking the halls before school started, hoping to see the robot in action. Unfortunately, Krysti was not just slowing Max down but also driving her crazy.

"Seriously," continued Krysti, "this school is already mega overrun with robots. Janitors, lunch ladies, librarians—all robots!"

"Krysti," said Max, "it is not just *another* robot. This is an artificially intelligent, fully—"

"If it's already so smart, then why is it going to school?" asked Jack Biggs, who had come up behind them.

This time Max definitely growled. It was bad enough listening to Krysti, who was supposedly her best friend, but Biggs was basically her best enemy. He always tried to hang around them, but then constantly picked on them—especially Max. It was maddening.

"Yeah," said Krysti, who tolerated Biggs much better than Max did. "It's supposed to be this big-deal super-smart robot and it has to take seventh-grade math?"

"Well, even geniuses like myself have to take seventh-grade math at some point," said Biggs.

"Hey, where are you guys going?" said Jack's sidekick, Simeon, as he approached them.

"Oh, Maxine is totally on the hunt for that robot," said Krysti. She gave the back of Max's head an affectionate tap with her ever-present sketchbook.

"Yeah, it's her best chance of getting a boyfriend," said Biggs.

Why me? thought Max. *Why do the three weirdest kids in the whole school always hang around me?*

But deep down, Max had to admit she felt closer to these three than to anybody else at the school. And she realized that she herself might very well be the fourth weirdest.

Then she saw a commotion up ahead. The robot must be up there.

She moved faster.

She didn't want the others to ruin this moment, and she wasn't going to let a gaggle of onlookers get in her way. Sure, everyone wanted to see the robot, but she wanted to see it more, so she zigged and zagged through the swarm of kids to get a look . . .

And then, there it was!

The robot!

Walking right toward her.

It looked absolutely ridiculous. It was only a little taller than Simeon—who was the shortest kid at Vanguard— and was dressed in boys' clothes at least five years out of style, and was wearing a dark wig.

And its face was . . . kind of creepy. The features were all there, but different. The bright blue eyes never blinked, the eyebrows looked as though they were painted on, the mouth was a closed straight line, and the nose was formed by straight planes that made its tip look pointed.

A lot of people were laughing at it, but Max thought, *That's just the way they dressed it. It can't help what it looks like. The important thing is that this is one of the most advanced robots on the planet, and it's right here where I can—*

And then it fell over.

Max actually had to jump back so it didn't land on her foot.

KLOMP! It must weigh a ton, she realized. It would have crushed her toes!

And then it just lay there. Frozen. Completely still. Bricked.

"Nice work," said Biggs, catching up from behind. "You already broke it, Max."

THE ROBOT DID APPEAR TO BE broken. It just lay there like a big toy someone had dropped. And somehow she felt like it *might* be her fault!

Can this day get any worse? she wondered.

Then the walls lit up. The computer-generated face of Vice Principal Barbara looked down on them from every angle.

Vice Principal Barbara was the school's supercomputer. She ran everything and kept an electronic eye on everything as well. And when she needed to communicate with the students, she had an on-screen avatar, which looked just like a grandmother . . . a sort of crazy grandmother. Sometimes friendly, sometimes stern, sometimes angry, and often flipping between these modes when least expected.

Right now, she was in what Biggs called "grumpy grandmother mode." To which Simeon had added, "You mean, Big Brother's Grumpy Grandmother." But they didn't say these things at school, where Barbara might hear them, of course.

"Please keep the hallways clear and safe," Barbara said, the mouth of her avatar slightly out of sync with her words. "No stopping is allowed in the hallways. Clear the way."

"But, Vice Principal Barbara," said Max. "The robot just fell down and—"

"Discipline tags will be assigned in five seconds," said Barbara. "Proceed to homeroom. Please keep the hallways clear and safe."

Krysti, Biggs, Simeon, and the other students immediately headed to class, though many craned their necks to look back at Max and the dead robot.

"But—" said Max.

"Discipline tag assigned to Student M. Zelaster," said Barbara.

Has it been five seconds already? wondered Max, but

she knew better than to wonder out loud, because that would probably get her an additional dTag.

She looked down at the still robot, reluctant to leave it. Maybe she could help?

"Don't touch it!" called a voice.

Max looked up to see three adults running down the hall. Robotics technicians. Max was dying to ask them questions.

"No running is allowed in the hallways at any time for any reason!" boomed Barbara, switching into *really* stern grandma mode. "Discipline tags assigned to School Visitor number 5, School Visitor number 8, School Visitor number 11. Your violation of school rules will be reported to your employer, Rossum Technologies. Additional discipline tag assigned to Student M. Zelaster. Clear the hallways. Please keep the hallways clean and safe."

Max didn't stick around to hear the rest. She headed for class before she got hit with any more dTags. She already had *way* too many.

OH MAN," SAID BIGGS. "GOOD-BYE, Robot Integration Program. I told you anything with the initials RIP was doomed. Rest in Peace, RIP!"

Yes, thought Max, *he did tell us that . . . about fifty times.*

"Those technicians looked pretty mad," said Simeon.

"Yeah," said Krysti, "they came running up, 'Don't touch it! Don't touch it!' Did they think you were going to give it mouth-to-mouth or something?"

"Yeah," repeated Biggs, way too loud—as usual. "And then Max goes—"

Luckily, Max didn't have to hear anymore, because a tone sounded over the loudspeakers, their desks lit up, and their science and homeroom teacher, Ms. French, said: "Now, I know there was a lot of excitement in the hall this morning. But we can't let it get us off track. This week's UpGrade testing is just around the corner, whether there's a robot in school or not. I suggest you use your homeroom time to review."

Ugh, thought Max. Reviewing for an UpGrade test was about the last thing she wanted to do. But sometimes it felt like it was the only thing she ever did. The tests were in every class, every week. And you had better make sure your UpGrade level never went down!

Everything at this school was focused on UpGrading. It was all part of a new Federal School Board program called Constant UpGrade. (Although the students had their own names for it.)

The Constant UpGrade program was supposed to be a "revolution in education" with "cutting-edge technology" like Barbara. But it had turned out to mostly be a giant pain in the butt. The cutting-edge technology was always yelling at you, and with the constant testing, none of the classes were any fun.

Since teachers got their own #CUG scores, all they seemed to care about was preparing for the next test.

And making it all even worse, parents received constant updates on everything from their child's test scores to dTags. Bomb a test or do something dumb and Barbara would be sure your parents heard about it in real time.

Vanguard did have a human principal, Mr. Dorgas, but everyone said—whispered, actually—that Barbara was really in charge. And they were right. She wasn't just running the school. She WAS the school.

Everything—every door, every camera, every screen, every sensor—was connected into the central computer running the Barbara software. All the janitor and lunchroom robots were under her control, plus dozens of others the students never saw, such as qScreen repairbots, heating duct cleaners, and dumpsterdroids, all rolling around on wheels or treads and mostly consisting of metallic appendages designed for their specific functions.

The goal of #CUG was a perfect school—higher test scores, fewer discipline problems, and cheaper to run.

Every part of the school must be Constantly UpGrading—the students, the teachers, the "learning materials," the robots, the flow of traffic in the halls, attendance, physical education achievements, proper hand-washing in the restrooms.

Barbara gave everything a #CUG score, and that #CUG score needed to keep going up. Anything other than a constant upgrade in your Constant UpGrade score meant trouble.

Every student's #CUG score was recalculated in real time. Attendance, discipline, and citizenship points were added or subtracted instantly. Homework was graded by computer, and students' #CUG scores were adjusted within the first minute of class.

And once a week came those Live UpGrade Assessments. They were really just multiple-choice tests, but they had a big and immediate impact on every student's #CUG score . . . and on the teachers' scores, too.

And it was working! Vanguard was exceeding all of its Constant UpGrade goals. Academic test scores were way up—actually, the highest of any school in Florida— and discipline problems were way down. In fact, almost nonexistent.

Although Vanguard still had human teachers and a

human principal, the Barbara system kept finding ways to replace more and more of the school's staff, saving even more taxpayer dollars.

Already there were plans to open up other Constant UpGrade schools with their own Barbara systems across the country.

Because the students under the Constant UpGrade system really were being constantly upgraded . . . according to Barbara's data.

CONSTANT UPGRADE DIDN'T just cause Max trouble at school. The computer system's instant communication with her parents often meant that she'd come home to find them all worked up about something that was really nothing.

And today was no exception.

Don and Carmen Zelaster had received texts about Max's two discipline tags, along with a reminder that Max needed to study for the weekly UpGrade test.

So she tried to explain the whole scene with the robot to her parents, but that just made it worse, because her mother did not share Max's interest in robots. In fact, ever since she and their city's other police dispatchers had lost their jobs to a computerized communications system, she had become anti-computer, anti-robot, and, Max thought, anti-everything. Now she was working at a small local library, downloading e-books for its patrons—at least until some robot took over there, too.

"I don't understand it," Carmen Zelaster said. "You just step over the robot and you go to class. End of story. No discipline tags. How hard is that?"

"I couldn't just leave him there—"

"'Him'? Honey, robots aren't 'hims,'" Max's mom said, clearly struggling to hold on to her patience. "They aren't 'hers.' They're machines. And if people start treating them like people, then we're really screwed. Just today I was reading about that failed Mars mission. The robot crashed the ship and it was just lucky there were no people abooard. Because, listen: They don't treat us like people. We're nothing more than just another machine to them, and once they're in charge—"

"Do we have to go into this again?" Don Zelaster interrupted quietly.

"It's important," said Max's mom.

"I know it is, but so is her test on Friday. If she does as badly as she did last week, her . . . uh . . . #CUG score is going to drop again, and she's *really* going to be in trouble!"

"She sure is!" agreed her mom. "Maxine, you—"

"So, that's why she needs to go study," said her dad firmly, and Max was grateful.

She didn't know how to talk to her mom about anything anymore, and her test scores were a particularly touchy subject. She *had* studied for the test last week. And the ones before it. And she thought she had done pretty well on them. She couldn't understand her poor performances.

But whenever Max tried telling that to her mother, she would just get angry and snap, "Well, you better figure it out!"

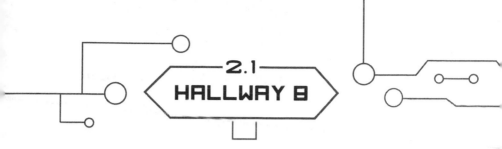

BACK AT SCHOOL THE NEXT DAY, Max was hoping to see the robot. But she ran into her friends instead, and apparently they were not done teasing her about yesterday's run-in with the robot.

"Hey, Max, where's your boyfriend?" Biggs asked.

"I heard they're packing him and all the equipment up and leaving," said Simeon with a superior smirk.

"Aw! What a bummer . . . I thought he was kind of cute," said Krysti, holding up a sketch she had done of the robot lying flat on his face.

Max didn't say anything. She was worried that Simeon was right. However, Simeon was famous for his exaggerated and often just plain false factoids, so she wasn't sure what to think.

All of a sudden there was a little *bing-bong* sound, and everybody froze. The notes on the big learning screen at the front of the room faded out, and the principal's face appeared. Everyone relaxed. If it was an important message, it would have been Barbara. This was just Mr. Dorgas.

Dorgas was a grumpy little man whom everybody called Dorkus, including some of the teachers when they thought no kids were listening.

"Maxine Zelaster, report to the office, please," he said.

All the other students in the room turned to stare at Max.

"Sounds gnarly," whispered Krysti, although her uncharacteristic frown showed she was worried for her friend. "What'd you do?"

"Nothing!" Max then appealed to their homeroom teacher: "Ms. French! This isn't fair. I haven't done anything wrong."

"Nobody said you did," said Ms. French, "but you can't ignore Dork—er, Mr. Dorgas. I suggest you hurry so you get back in time for the UpGrade review."

So Max hurried, walking as fast as she could without running. No reason to rack up another dTag.

She was almost to the office when a long durafoam arm sprang out of the wall and blocked her way. She knew from experience that, if she tried to go around or under it, it would extend a durafoam band that would actually encircle her and hold her in place.

A large section of wall lit up, showing Vice Principal Barbara looking firm but not yet angry.

"Discipline tag assigned to Student M. Zelaster. You are not authorized for this hallway at this time."

"But, Vice Principal Barbara, I've been called to the office!" Max protested.

"No record found," said Barbara, and the screen image became slightly grumpier. "You are not authorized for this hallway at this time."

A keypad appeared on the touch screen.

"Press one to review hallway procedures. Press two to—"

Max was actually considering trying to duck under the arm and make a run for it when Mr. Dorgas came around the corner.

"There you are, Zelaster! Follow me."

"I can't," she protested. "Vice Principal Barbara won't let me."

"Oops," said Dorgas, like it was no big deal. "I forgot to key you in. Barbara: Override, code seven."

The arm disappeared into the wall with a *whoosh*, and Max wished she could, too. Dorkus seemed to be in his usual bad mood. He stalked off down the hall, and she followed him.

"You know," he said, "if you didn't have so many discipline tags, Barbara wouldn't be on the lookout for you."

Max wanted to point out that if Barbara didn't have so many annoying rules, she wouldn't have so many dTags. But saying so might mean another tag, and it really wasn't worth it.

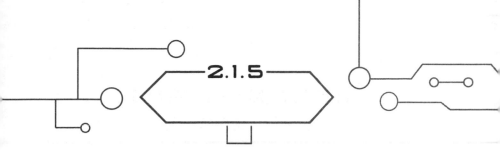

2.1.5

MEANWHILE, BARBARA WAS adding a discipline tag to Max's record anyway. She also added one to her internal record of Mr. Dorgas. Barbara kept careful track of every human who disputed her rules in any way.

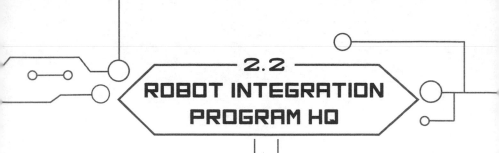

MR. DORGAS LED MAX TO A door marked FORUM, a mini-auditorium meant for school choral concerts and plays. But Vanguard had done away with music and drama classes, so the room was never used.

Now there was a little sign taped to the wall. ROBOT INTEGRATION PROGRAM HEADQUARTERS. ROSSUM TECHNOLOGIES. AUTHORIZED PERSONNEL ONLY.

When Mr. Dorgas hit the button, the door swooshed open and Max saw what looked to her like paradise.

Computers and vid screens and wires and spare parts filled the space, and in the middle of it all, she saw the robot.

Her first thought was *Oh cool,* but then she realized

it was just propped up against a table, not moving. So her second thought was *Oh zark, it's still broken. Maybe Biggs was right and I really did break it somehow.*

"Here is the student you requested, Dr. Jones," said Mr. Dorgas, and he pushed Max forward. Then he turned around and stomped out the door.

Everybody in the room—seven technicians, four security guards, and two people wearing weird helmets—turned to look at her.

One of the people in the weird helmets stepped forward.

"Uh . . . Maxine? Is that right?"

"Just Max, really," she said nervously.

The man pulled the helmet off over his head and introduced himself.

"I'm Dr. Jones, RosTech project manager." He was a lanky middle-aged white man with a receding hairline. Max noticed that he wore glasses. He must have been one of those rare types who couldn't tolerate ocular implants.

"And this," said Jones, waving at the other helmeted person, "is Lieutenant Colonel Nina."

A *colonel?* Max stepped back. Why would there be a

colonel here? Was she going to be some sort of gung ho army soldier who would yell at her for messing with the robot?

But when the "soldier" removed her helmet, Max saw that she was a friendly looking black woman, about thirty years old, with a nice, reassuring smile. She looked more like somebody's cool aunt than a soldier.

The woman gave Max another pleasant smile, and Max found herself smiling back.

"Hi, Max. Jones has to call me Lieutenant Colonel, but you can call me Nina."

"Hi, Nina," said Max. "It's nice to—"

"Right," interrupted Jones. "And this is my team . . ." He gestured at the technicians—brainy-looking twenty-somethings, mostly—who had come forward to meet Max. "And they're all getting back to work, because we're on a very tight deadline and yesterday morning's failure sure didn't help."

The brainy-looking twenty-somethings slunk back to their qScreens.

Max's ears turned red.

"About yesterday morning," she said. "I didn't mean to—"

"Oh, we know that," said Nina.

"Is the robot OK? Did I break it somehow . . . ?"

"Break it?" Nina laughed. "Max, you couldn't break Fuzzy with a bulldozer."

"Fuzzy?" asked Max, getting less worried but more confused.

And then came a third voice:

"I am Fuzzy. Hello, Object 321."

Max looked at the robot, but it didn't appear to have spoken. It didn't even appear to be turned on. It was still leaning against the table, not moving.

"Uh, was that the robot?" she asked, unsure of whom to talk to.

"Yes," said the voice again.

Then she noticed another head nearby. This one looked less human at first, but then she realized it was just missing the wig.

"Uh, which head is talking?" asked Max.

Nina let out another laugh. "Oh, I think Fuzzy's voice is coming from the speakers on that qScreen right now. When he's running again, his voice should come from the head attached to his body. That other one is just a backup."

"A backup head?" asked Max.

"Yeah, life with Fuzzy takes a little getting used to. He's more than an ordinary robot, but he's definitely not a flesh-and-blood human, either."

"And its name is Fuzzy?"

"Yes, my name is Fuzzy," said the voice again.

"Why do you call it Fuzzy?" Max asked Nina.

"Do you like it?" asked Nina, smiling. "I named him. His real name is—"

"Classified!" interjected Jones.

Nina rolled her eyes.

"Classified?" asked Max. "Why would it be classified?"

"Ha! Well, the reason it's classified is also classified," said Nina.

Max felt more confused than she had ever been in her life.

"Basically," explained Nina, "the government wants a smarter robot, so we've hired Jones and his team to create Fuzzy."

Then Nina leaned in close to Max and, rolling her eyes again, said in a loud whisper, "They're civilians."

"You still haven't told her why you named it Fuzzy," said Jones.

"I was about to when you interrupted me!" Nina

said with mock outrage. Jones and Nina were starting to remind Max of her grandparents. They must have been working together for so long they were like an old married couple.

"Anyway . . . ," continued Nina, "we call him Fuzzy because he is designed to use fuzzy logic. Have you heard of that?"

"Uh, yeah," said Max. "Isn't that the thing where two plus two isn't always four?"

"Sort of," said Nina. "Basically, most robots and computers are programmed to calculate, or even to analyze, but not to really think. We're trying to create a robot that thinks for himself. So he has to figure out for himself what two plus two is."

"Tutu," said Fuzzy.

Max found herself grinning. "Was that a joke? Does it tell jokes?"

"We're not exactly sure yet. We're still trying to understand him," said Nina. "By the way, please feel free to talk to Fuzzy directly."

"He's one of the most advanced robots ever created," said Jones. "State-of-the-art speech recognition and language processors, plus we've loaded several slang and idiom databases to help him talk to you kids. So, if you speak clearly, he'll understand you most of the time."

"Hello, uh, Fuzzy?" said Max, still completely unsure where to look.

"Hello, Object 321," said Fuzzy.

"Oh, uh . . . I think that's you," Nina told Max.

"What? I'm an object? Or is that another joke?"

"Well, no," said Nina. "We have turned off some of his nonessential programs. The name database must be part of that."

"Yes. Fuzzy's sort of in recovery mode right now," said Dr. Jones, a hand brushing at his nonexistent hair. "We had a little problem yesterday, as you probably saw when you approached him."

"Oh zark . . . ," Max began. "Like I said, I hope I didn't—"

"No, no, it's OK," Nina quickly reassured her. "It wasn't you. We know exactly what happened— Well, sort of. We've just been watching you on the playback. These helmets let us see whatever Fuzzy sees and does. We're still trying to figure out why he fell."

"Would you like to try it out?" asked Dr. Jones.

Max couldn't believe it: She didn't seem to be in

trouble, and it looked like she was going to get to play with the stuff! The helmet was a NebulonVirtX—a virtual reality device. Insanely expensive. She had only read about them on the net. She had never seen one.

"Absolutely!" she said. "But why me?"

"I'm not exactly sure," said Jones. "But Fuzzy asked us to find you and ask for your help."

"*My* help?" asked Max. "I mean, yeah, sure, I'd love to . . . but what can I do?"

"Well," said Nina, "have you ever heard that thing about walking in someone else's shoes so you can understand them?"

"Um, I guess . . . ," said Max.

"Well, with Fuzzy's technology you can actually do that."

Nina carefully eased the helmet down over Max's head and onto her shoulders.

"Uh, it's all black."

"It hasn't started yet," said Jones. "OK, Fuzzy, playback from mark eighty-three."

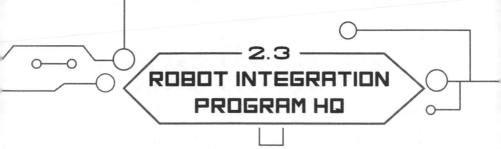

WHAT MAX SAW ALMOST MADE her freak out. There seemed to be numbers and words floating everywhere, right in front of her. They looked like the imaging on qGoggles run amok.

After a few seconds she realized what she was seeing. It was a 3-D display showing a fully dimensional video of the hallway, with kids pushing and shoving past. And each kid had a bunch of numbers floating over his or her head. Then she saw herself zooming toward the viewer, weaving in and out of other kids' paths, until she filled the screen.

Over her head it said:

```
Hallway.obj.321
Vel.34.2, 0, 22.43
Face.Recog: processing . . .
```

Meanwhile, words scrolled over all this like movie credits on very fast-forward:

```
Obj.avoidance(320) processing . . .
Find.path(a*) processing . . .
Right.leg(forward, speed:10.87543)
Obj.avoidance(321) processing . . .
Record.data.obj.321
Find.path(a*) processing . . .
Right.leg(back, speed:6.987654)
Balance.check() null pointer returned
```

Then it went black again.

She pulled off the helmet.

"Is that what Fuzzy sees? No wonder he fell over."

She was surprised to see that both Jones and Nina were watching her intently.

"Exactly," said Jones. "That's why we need your help."

"I need a new hallway navigation program" came Fuzzy's slightly mechanical, disembodied voice again.

"Well," said Max, "I can do a little programming, mostly Nix++ and some Nextran, but . . ."

"Oh, don't worry about that," said Nina. "Fuzzy can reprogram himself."

"Obviously," said Jones, "it would be no big deal to program a robot to follow a path from point A to point B, but navigating a hall full of kids is much more complicated. The point with Fuzzy is that he doesn't *need* to be preprogrammed. He can figure things out for himself and then constantly update his programming to get better and better."

"Right," said Nina. "So, eventually he would learn how to get through the halls here—even when they are packed with a bunch of crazy kids—but we can't have him out there falling down again and again."

"And we're on a tight deadline," interjected Jones. "We need to get on to the big stuff."

"Right," Nina said again. "The big stuff—going to classes, meeting the other students, and so on. That's what we're really here for. So he needs someone to quickly teach him how to get through the halls, and we noticed on the vid that you do it pretty well."

"You were great, Object 321," said Fuzzy. "I saw you weaving through the crowd. But you never bumped into anyone. You understand how hallway navigation works. You can help me."

Max didn't think her hallway survival skills were any better than anybody else's. But it would be crazy to tell them she couldn't help . . . because she really wanted to. And yet it felt a little like she was getting her driver's chip early. Sure, she'd love to drive a car, but shouldn't she get a lesson or something first?

"What if I try to help but he ends up falling over again?" she asked. "What if I break him?"

Dr. Jones laughed. "He's designed to survive a lot, even something as rough as landing on another planet— or, I mean, some really rugged place like that. We've had him walk through two deserts, a jungle, and a mountain range. So I don't think you can damage him. Just help him figure out the little stuff, and if any big stuff happens, we're monitoring everything and we'll be right there."

"Will you do it, Object 321?" asked Fuzzy.

"Yeah, sure, I'll try. But, please, just call me Max."

"One second, Object 321."

There was a long pause. Longer than one second. Then, so suddenly that she jumped, the robot came to life. He walked across the floor and held out his hand. She put out hers, and the robot shook it. His hand wasn't cold as she had expected.

"Thank you, Max," the robot said.

Max smiled. "The first thing I need to teach you, Fuzzy," she said, "is that only old people shake hands."

2.4
HALLWAY B

HAT RULES DO YOU USE TO walk down the hall?" Fuzzy asked.

"Rules?" Max mumbled. "Uh . . ."

Fuzzy, Jones, and Nina all stood there looking at her, and she had no idea what sort of rules there could be for walking down a hall, other than not shoving anyone and not falling down. Then she remembered how Fuzzy had been running that face recognition routine when he crashed.

"First of all, don't try to recognize everybody's faces this time. Trust me, it's all just going to be a big blur."

"OK, Max, I will turn the facial recognition software off again. But I will create a special subroutine to recognize you."

"Wow, thanks," said Max, genuinely pleased. "A subroutine just for me! I guess that's the robot equivalent of becoming friends."

(Jones and Nina decided not to mention that Fuzzy had millions of subroutines, which are just small programs that a computer can call on to do a specific job and then turn off when the job is done.)

"OK," Max was saying. "I thought of a rule: Don't walk along next to the wall, because you'll just get blocked by the water fountains."

"Do you know what brand the water fountains are?"

"Uh, what? No, why?"

"I am going to download their dimensions and add them to my WallAvoidance() subroutine."

"Uh, I wouldn't worry about it," she said. "You know, I think maybe we're making this too complicated. Maybe if you come to class with me, you can just follow me down the hall and see what I do."

"Great," said Nina, "that's exactly what we're hoping for. Why don't you go to your next class? If he makes it, great. If not, we'll be about twenty feet behind you."

Then a bell rang.

"Uh-oh . . . I'm going to have to go kind of fast," said Max. "You ready?"

Dr. Jones looked a little unsure. "Perhaps we should . . . um . . ."

But Fuzzy said, "I am ready, Max," and they took off.

"Remember, we're behind you in case anything goes wrong!" called Nina. "Fuzzy . . . be careful!"

How embarrassing, thought Max. *Poor Fuzzy. Nina's like a kindergarten mom.*

FUZZY OBEDIENTLY ADJUSTED his settings to use extra caution.

The hallway was packed as everyone went from homeroom to first period. It was twice as crazy as Fuzzy's last hallway trip.

"Just keep behind me," said Max, "and I'll plow a path."

Fuzzy noticed that she didn't exactly *plow* a path. Sometimes kids moved out of her way, and sometimes she moved out of their way. He recorded some data on all this so that he could run simulations later. But mostly he just tried to stay right behind Max, without stepping on her.

Max stopped suddenly, and Fuzzy, with a reaction time much faster than any human, instantly stopped, too. He shifted slightly to see what was in front of Max that had made her stop.

It was Object 429, a large male human.

"Max! It's right behind you!" the male object said.

"Yeah, Biggs, it's right behind me," Max said, imitating Object 429's tone. Fuzzy detected that she appeared uncomfortable with the encounter, perhaps because other kids were staring at them now. "Listen, I'll introduce you later. We got to get to class."

She sidestepped Object 429 and kept going. Fuzzy did the same thing—exactly.

"Wait! What is going on, Max?" hollered Biggs, and he started following her, too.

"Look, Biggs, it's not a parade," said Max, stopping again.

Fuzzy stopped instantly again, too, but Biggs didn't. He slammed right into Fuzzy.

Max cringed, expecting another robo-crash. But Fuzzy just made a bunch of little steps with his feet and stayed upright.

"Wow! This thing is pretty cool!" said Biggs. "Can I try to push it over?"

"Yes, Object 429, you may test my balancing capabilities."

"No!" said Max, jumping between them. She looked back to see if Jones and Nina were still nearby. They were, and Nina slipped up next to Max and whispered, "It's OK, we want to let Fuzzy interact with the other students. He'll be OK."

"So much for the kindergarten mom," Max said so softly that only Fuzzy's enhanced hearing picked it up. But she stepped back and said aloud, "All right, Biggs, go ahead and act like an idiot if you have to."

Biggs shoved Fuzzy as hard as he could. This time, Fuzzy didn't even make the tiny steps. He just shifted his weight into Biggs precisely enough to stay motionless.

"Wow!" said Biggs, rubbing his fingers.

"Threatening behavior identified," came a flat, grating female voice. Sure enough, Barbara's avatar popped up on the nearest wall screen, the extra-stern version this time.

"I wonder why she never sounds human like you do?" Max whispered to Fuzzy.

"I wasn't trying to hurt him!" pleaded Biggs to the screen. "He said I could! And so did that lady!"

"Vanguard Middle School has a zero tolerance policy regarding threatening behavior and physical contact. Tap the review button on my screen if you wish to review the policy."

"No, thanks," muttered Biggs.

"Discipline tags assigned to J. Biggs . . ."

Fuzzy detected an expression he would have called, from his studies of human expressions, a smirk on Max's face. Until the Barbara avatar kept going.

". . . M. Zelaster, and F. Robot."

"But we didn't . . . ," Max started to say, when a bell rang.

Max looked around. "Oh no! We're the only ones still in the hall."

"Tardiness tags assigned to J. Biggs, M. Zelaster, and F. Robot," continued Barbara. "Thirty seconds until violation is upgraded."

"*But—*" said Max and Biggs at the same time.

"Maybe you'd better go on to class," said Nina. "I didn't mean for you to get into trouble. I'll talk to your principal about it."

They walked down the hall in silence. Biggs was mad at Barbara. Max was mad at Barbara *and* Biggs. And Fuzzy was trying not to fall over.

THEY GOT TO THE DOOR AND it slid open, interrupting Ms. French, who had already started the UpGrade test review.

"I see you got to meet the new robot," Ms. French said.

"Yes, this is Fuzzy. Fuzzy, this is Ms. French."

"Hello, Ms. French," said Fuzzy.

Max was pleased to see that he didn't try to shake her hand or call her an object. He must have turned the face recognition back on. He was already learning how to be social.

"Well, um, hello, Fuzzy." Max could see that Ms. French, who was only about fifteen years older than her students, appeared to be stressed. Friendly but stressed. That was her usual look, actually.

"I wish there was time for the whole class to find out more about you, but I'm about to launch the review program for tomorrow's test. Do you need to sit down?"

"Do you wish me to sit down?"

"Yes, at that desk, please."

Ms. French waited until Fuzzy sat himself in a vacant aisle combo-desk and then gave a single hand clap, her signal for silence. "All right, class," she said. "If you'll turn back to your qScreens. Ralph, please read the question."

"List all planets, including the largest dwarf planets, in order of distance from the sun," Ralph said smugly, probably sure he could get this answer right.

"And can you name the planets, Ralph?" Ms. French asked.

"Mercury, Venus, Earth, Mars, Jupiter, Saturn, Uranus, Neptune, dwarf planet Pluto—"

"That is not correct, Ralph," said Fuzzy.

Uh-oh, thought Max, *Fuzzy still has a lot to learn.*

"Fuzzy!" she hissed. "You're not the teacher! Just sit there!"

"It's OK, Max," said Ms. French. "Fuzzy, I'm pretty sure I heard Ralph list the planets in the right order."

"At the moment, Pluto's orbit has brought it closer to the sun than Neptune," said Fuzzy.

"Do we need to know this for the test?" asked Krysti, whose mission in life was to never learn anything that wasn't going to be on a test.

"Well. That's very interesting, Fuzzy," broke in Ms. French. "I'm sure we will all be very interested to learn about this when we aren't preparing for the test."

"So we don't have to know it for the test?" asked Krysti.

"No, you don't," said Ms. French. "In fact, it'll be best if you forget it. The only answer that's going to count on tomorrow's UpGrade is the one Ralph gave. I'm sorry, Fuzzy."

"But shouldn't we learn the right answer?" asked Max.

"Maybe later," said Ms. French, and she turned toward a boy on the other side of the room. "Noa, perhaps you could read the next question for us."

"But it's silly to learn the wrong answer," insisted Max.

"Please, Max, can we discuss this later? We need to get through the rest of the review. Go ahead, Noa."

Max and Fuzzy sat silently for the rest of the class. Max scowled, but Fuzzy was expressionless. Max wondered what he was thinking. Then she realized she hadn't been paying attention to the review and groaned. She'd have to study extra-hard tonight.

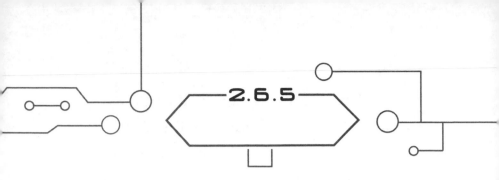

MEANWHILE, BARBARA—WHO HAD camera eyes in every classroom—had just given both Max and Fuzzy another discipline tag for distracting from the learning environment and had lowered Max's school citizen score several points for questioning the importance of UpGrading.

ON'T WORRY, FUZZY," SAID MAX as they walked down the hall. "Mr. Xu's class is gonna go much better."

"Yeah," said Simeon, who had joined a group following Max and Fuzzy down the hall. "Xu's really cool. He's going to think having a robot for a student is totally awesome!"

Max groaned. Simeon was another one of the old-fashioned slang users like Krysti. Plus, she was annoyed that Simeon was even there at all.

Max knew she should be glad that some of the other kids liked Fuzzy, too—after all, that was the whole point of a Robot Integration Program. But she couldn't help being a little irritated that they were all hanging around now. She'd hardly had a chance to talk to Fuzzy herself. And she had so many questions.

But this wasn't a great time to talk anyway, since Mr. Xu's class was in Hallway D and there was barely enough time to get there before the chime rang and Barbara started giving out discipline tags.

Mr. Xu was, in fact, very excited to meet Fuzzy.

"I'm sure everyone is as curious as I am. Would you mind answering some questions, Fuzzy?" he asked once the class was settled.

"No, I would not mind," said Fuzzy.

Lots of kids put their hands up, but Mr. Xu said he wanted to ask the first question. "How old are you?" he asked.

"My current software, Fuzzy.9, was turned on twenty-two days ago. However, I am aware of my previous actions and training since my central processors were brought online four hundred and eighty-three days ago."

"Let's see," said Mr. Xu. "Divide 483 by 365 and . . . So, you're about a year and a half old!"

"Correct," said Fuzzy.

"Fascinating," said Mr. Xu. "OK, who's got the next question?" Hands went up. "Simeon, go ahead."

"Do you use batteries or what?" asked Simeon.

"Yes. In fact, forty-five percent of my weight is batteries, stored here in my abdomen, pelvis, and thighs." Fuzzy pointed to his rear end and did not seem to mind everyone laughing at him.

"How long do they last?" asked Krysti.

So much for her not caring about robots, thought Max with a smile.

"An average of 55.3 hours," he said. "If I were, say, in a desert or on some other planet, I would have solar panels sent along with me to extend the time between recharges at a base station."

Biggs was in this class, too, and Max was completely unsurprised to hear him ask the dumbest question of all time: "Do you use the bathroom?"

Apparently Mr. Xu thought this was a dumb question, too, because he was just about to fuss at Biggs about it. But then they were all surprised when Fuzzy answered. "Yes. I have a coolant system to control the temperature of my processors. This creates condensation, or tiny water droplets, which collect in a short tube and must be emptied from time to time. A bathroom would be a convenient place for me to do so."

The few titters of laughter stopped when Mr. Xu tapped lightly on his desk.

"Can you send a text message?" asked Jenny, a girl who was usually too full of herself to take an interest in anything else.

"Yes," said Fuzzy.

"Will you send me one?" Jenny asked.

Fuzzy just sat there, and Max knew that somebody was going to start making fun of him in about half a second, when Jenny held up her qFlex bracelet. A text message was scrolling around the surface.

"Wow! How did you know my number?"

"I saw your name on your notebook."

Everyone looked and saw that it said *Jenny Turling* in tiny letters at the top of her notebook.

Fuzzy's eyes must be able to zoom in on stuff just like a camera, Max realized. Then she thought, *Duh, they* are *cameras!*

"And then," continued Fuzzy, "I accessed the databases of the major cell phone companies and found fifty-seven Jenny Turlings. But there is only one in this area."

"But aren't those databases private?" asked Max.

"Well, there is a primitive sort of password protection," replied Fuzzy, "but I decrypted it with—"

Suddenly, one of the big wall screens lit up with Vice Principal Barbara's virtual face.

"Unauthorized use of text-messaging device. One discipline tag to F. Robot. One discipline tag to J. Turling."

Jenny let out an indignant squawk and turned to Mr. Xu.

Mr. Xu gave her a little nod.

"Vice Principal Barbara, I think we can override those tags. The text message was part of a classroom demonstration," he said.

"There are no records that you made a request to violate school guidelines for such a demonstration," Barbara's grating voice replied.

"Well, it just came up. Now, Vice Principal Barbara, if—"

"I will make a note that allowing students to send text messages is one of your teaching methods. I am unaware of how it can be helpful in studying the history of colonial America, the subject of your upcoming UpGrade test. This information will be reflected in your Constant UpGrade teacher score." Her screen flicked off.

Mr. Xu looked like he was burning with a desire

to throw something heavy at Vice Principal Barbara's screen. But he no doubt knew from past experience that Barbara was still watching and, in fact, recording whatever he did next, ready to further reduce his #CUG score if he showed any reaction at all.

So, he took a deep breath. "Fuzzy, I'd like to thank you for answering our questions. I'm sure it will be a valuable experience for all of us to have you in our class. However, now I think it would be best for us to return to today's Constant UpGrade study schedule: Agricultural Methods of the 1700s."

3.2 CAFETERIA

AS THEY MADE THEIR WAY FROM history class to the cafeteria, Fuzzy walked steadily, with no trace of his troubles from the day before. He seemed just like any other kid. Krysti, in fact, seemed to have accepted him as just one of the gang and was chattering away as usual.

"Did you see Mr. Xu's face?" she asked. "He was buggin' big-time."

"Buggin' . . . big . . . time . . . ?" said Biggs. "Fuzzy here probably thinks you're speaking Norwegian or something."

"Actually," said Fuzzy. "I understand both the Norwegian language and the slang terms that Krysti is using. "'Buggin' big-time' is a combination of two popular colloquial phrases from the late twentieth century: 'bugging' meaning to lose control of one's emotions and 'big-time' meaning 'very much so.'"

"Whoa! Thanks, Fuzz!" said Krysti, and she threw her arm around him like they were best friends. "You're cooler than you look! Speaking of which, I think I'm going to draw your picture during lunch."

"You should have him fighting a monster like a movie robot," suggested Biggs.

"Fuzzy versus Godzilla!" yelled Simeon.

Max was annoyed.

She hoped that once they sat down for lunch she'd finally have a chance to really talk to Fuzzy. But almost as soon as they walked into the cafeteria, he started slowing down. Max guided him over to their table, and then he just sort of sat there. He wouldn't answer anyone's questions, and he hardly moved.

"I bet his batteries ran down," said Biggs.

"No way, bro. They last for 55.3 hours without recharging," said Simeon with that know-it-all tone of his that really drove Max nuts.

"Fuzzy, I wanted you to pose, dude," said Krysti, holding up her sketchbook.

But Fuzzy still just sat there.

Then Dr. Jones and a couple of technicians with a motorized cart showed up.

Max panicked. What had she done wrong?

"I'm sorry, Dr. Jones! I don't know what happened."

"It's not your fault, Max," said Jones. "I should have anticipated this. I just forgot how crazy school cafeterias are."

"'Crazy'?" said Krysti. "It's totally boring."

"It may be boring to you," said Dr. Jones, "but I can barely hear myself think in here. There must be two hundred kids talking at once. In fact, look at this . . ."

He held out a book-size qScreen showing hundreds of lines of computer code on its LCD screen.

"Make that two hundred and fifty-seven," said Jones.

The code looked like gibberish to most of the kids, but now Max knew what to look for.

```
SpeechRecog(stream(254))
SpeechRecog(stream(255))
SpeechRecog(stream(256))
SpeechRecog(stream(257))
```

"Smoke!" she said. "He was trying to understand everything everybody in the whole cafeteria was saying at the same time."

"We'll take him back to the room for a reboot for now," said Jones. "And then we'll either have to turn off his voice recognition when he comes in here or figure out some way for him to listen to just one person at a time."

The technicians loaded Fuzzy onto the cart and wheeled him away.

Dr. Jones stayed long enough to say to Max, "You gonna help us again tomorrow?"

"You mean, I can? I thought you'd be mad that I let him freeze up again!"

"No, no," assured Jones. "You did a great job with him, Max. And we could definitely use your help again tomorrow . . ."

"You got it!"

THE NEXT DAY WENT A LOT smoother.

Fuzzy went to all of Max's morning classes and then turned his voice recognition subroutines off as they walked into the cafeteria. Max and the other kids were able to write notes to him on their qFlex bracelets, and then he could read their questions and answer normally.

Of course, it's hard to call any answer "normal" when the question—from Simeon, of course—was: "Could you kill Godzilla?"

After lunch, Max had gym. She wasn't sure what to do about Fuzzy. She knew she couldn't bring him into the girl's locker room. But then she wondered why not. He wasn't really a boy or a girl, just a robot. Then she thought about Fuzzy seeing her dressing for gym and knew that absolutely no way could he go in there.

She stopped before turning down the hall to the gym.

"Uh, Fuzzy, you better ask Dr. Jones what to do about gym class. I can't take you with me into the locker room."

"Why not, Max? Are you afraid I'll see you in your underwear?"

Max turned bright red and her ears turned even redder. How could he know about underwear? Could he have been making a joke?

Before she could think of anything to say, Fuzzy had sent a text message to Dr. Jones and gotten one back.

Fuzzy wasn't allowed in gym class for safety reasons. Dr. Jones wanted Max to drop Fuzzy off at the tech room.

Max looked at the time on her qFlex. Great. She would *really* have to hustle to drop off Fuzzy and get back to the gym on time. But she couldn't just ditch him.

"C'mon, Fuzz, we've got to hurry."

She sped up and started weaving past clumps of

slow-moving kids in the hallway. Fuzzy kept up with no problem. He was apparently learning that you didn't have to watch every kid, just the clumps.

When they got to the tech room, she was ready to say good-bye to Fuzzy and hightail it to gym. But Dr. Jones and Nina wanted to talk.

"We are really impressed with the progress Fuzzy has been making," said Nina.

"Do you know he has written eighty thousand lines of new code today?" asked Jones.

"That's good, right?" asked Max, anxious to get out of there.

"Yes, that's what he's here for," said Dr. Jones. "Unfortunately, we just learned today that his launch date—that is, the time when we need him to be fully activated—has been moved up. We won't have as much time as we had hoped. So we need to do everything we can to keep him learning."

"How would you feel about spending some time with Fuzzy after school?" asked Nina.

"Uh, you mean like a study hall?"

"No, we mean away from school," Nina said.

"You don't mean like a date?" gasped Max. She thought about how Krysti and, of course, Biggs, were already teasing her about her robot boyfriend.

"Well, no, nothing like a date," said Dr. Jones. "But how about taking him home for dinner? He can ride the bus with you."

"Ride the bus? But what if—"

"Don't worry," said Nina. "We'll follow along, of course, with a couple of security units. But we want him to have as many typical kid experiences as possible. When you get to your house, we'll wait outside in case there are any problems. You'll have a chance to talk more and help him figure out this whole school thing. Then we'll bring him back here."

"Uh . . . I guess," Max said. "Listen, I've really got to go now. I'll be back after gym class."

She bolted from the room, but had barely started down the hall when the chime rang. And then came a voice she had heard way too much lately:

"Late for class. One discipline tag to M. Zelaster."

YOU MIGHT AT LEAST HAVE messaged first," said Max's father. "I'd have ordered pizza or something . . ."

"Dad, don't worry about it. Fuzzy doesn't eat," Max said.

"Oh. That's right. Of course not." Don Zelaster smacked his forehead in a *Duh!* gesture. "But still . . ." He looked to where Fuzzy was scanning a bookshelf in the next room, apparently out of earshot. Max wondered if Fuzzy knew what a book was. Old-fashioned books were one of her mother's affectations.

"It may not sit too well with your mom, you know," her dad said in a lower voice. "I think she made her feelings about robot students pretty clear the other day. And now you've actually brought the thing home . . ."

"Oh zar—er, smoke," said Max. She stopped herself because her father still considered "zark" a bad word. *But, really,* thought Max, *this is a totally zarked situation.*

She had gotten so used to Fuzzy already that she hadn't been thinking about what her mom's reaction would be. And it would almost certainly be bad.

"OK," she said, "but I wish you wouldn't call him a 'thing.'"

Her father shook his head. "Isn't this the exact same conversation you had with your mother? Do you really want to get her all riled up again? And besides . . . it *is* a thing. A thing with a bad wig."

Max groaned.

"He's not—"

"Trust me, honey, I know what I am saying," said her dad, who, in fact, did know a lot about robots because of his job writing high-tech instruction manuals. "I know it can seem real, but that's because some company spent a lot of money to preprogram it to seem that way. Believe me. I just finished an instruction manual for a very friendly blender."

Max rolled her eyes. If her father was having this much attitude about Fuzzy, she could hardly imagine what her mother was going to be like. Actually, she *could* imagine . . . and she knew she would rather avoid it altogether.

"I'll get Fuzzy to call Jones and cut the visit short," Max whispered to her father.

"I think that would be a good idea . . . and *quickly,* since Mom is due home from the library any minute now," her father agreed. "Your mother has many virtues, honey. But love of technology isn't one of them."

Max went through the kitchen to the living room, where Fuzzy was still standing before the bookcase. "Uh, Fuzzy, I hate to rush you off, but maybe we'd better get you back to your people . . ."

"Of course, Max," Fuzzy promptly agreed, and turned with her to the door. "It was interesting to meet you, Mr. Zelaster," he said to Max's father as they passed by him.

"It was interesting to meet you, too, Fuzzy." He smiled at the robot, and Max could tell he was charmed by Fuzzy's good manners. "You're even better than the SwirlTec190," her dad called as they continued through the front door.

Once they were outside, Max stopped and turned to Fuzzy. "You heard everything Dad and I were saying in there, didn't you?"

It was fascinating to see a robot hesitate. Max felt as though she could almost hear gears and circuits whirring somewhere inside Fuzzy.

"Yes," he finally admitted.

"Fuzzy! You're not supposed to listen to conversations like that!"

"I cannot tone down my hearing. And unless I turn off voice recognition ahead of time, I cannot help but understand what is said. And I cannot know what type of conversation it is unless I have voice recognition on."

Fuzzy stopped talking, but Max didn't speak because she could tell he was thinking of what to say next. *It must be pretty complicated if it's taking him more than a millisecond to figure out,* she thought.

"Max, I apologize if I have upset you."

"No, I didn't want you to apologize. I am just sorry that you heard all of that. I hope it didn't—" Now it was her turn to hesitate. She was about to say "I hope it didn't hurt your feelings," but she realized that that was ridiculous. Or was it?

"I hope it didn't interfere with your . . . uh . . . integration."

"No. This has been very useful," said Fuzzy.

"Well . . . good, I guess," said Max. "I'm sorry we're not being very polite, but, you see, my mom would blow a gasket if—"

"Max!"

It was her mom . . . and it sounded like she had blown a gasket already.

66

4.2
THE FRONT LAWN

ER MOM WAS YELLING FROM inside a silent solar car, which had just eased to a stop in front of their house.

"Will you unlock the door, you stupid thing!" she yelled at the car. One of her least favorite things about these automated PubliCars was the weird pause between their stopping and the unlocking of the doors.

When she finally got out, she slammed the door shut and stomped across the yard as the car eased back onto the traffic grid.

"Zarking PubliCars . . . I remember when we had real cars . . . ," she muttered.

When she finally got over to Max and Fuzzy, she

completely ignored Fuzzy and started right in on Max.

"Young lady, what's your excuse for all these discipline tags you racked up today? They've piled up to the point where I even got a phone call at work this afternoon. Not just the normal text messages but an actual call from somebody at the Federal School Board!"

"What on earth is going on?" asked her dad from the front doorway.

"Haven't you heard about all of her discipline tags today?"

"No, I wasn't checking my phone. Maxine, why didn't you tell me?"

Oh zark, thought Max, *this is getting out of hand.* Her parents were acting like it was the end of the world, and she couldn't even remember what she'd done wrong.

"I—I—I didn't know," she stammered. "I mean, I knew I got one for being late to class, but that was a mistake. Dorgas was supposed to—"

"Late to class? Oh, no! That was just for starters. The lady had a whole list: ignoring rules, breaking rules, classroom disruption, bad attitude, and something called 'stubborn willfulness.'"

"Stubborn willfulness?" Max yelped. "What the heck is that? Mom . . ."

"Carmen," said her father, "can we finish this discussion inside . . . where the neighbors won't hear the whole thing?"

"Good idea," said her mom, moving toward the door. "Because . . ."

Her voice trailed off as she noticed Fuzzy for the first time.

"What in thunderation is this?" she demanded.

"Inside, please, inside," said Max's father.

"*Well?*" said her mother once they were all in the house.

"Hello, Ms. Zelaster," Fuzzy said just as calmly as he'd have said it if he wasn't being yelled at. "My name is Fuzzy. I am one of the students at your daughter's school."

"A robot? You have *got* to be kidding me! What on earth is it doing here?"

Max's father tried to calm things down. "They thought

that it might help him to go home with a student, and Max was—"

"*Him?*"

"Uh . . . Max, I thought you were calling them to pick him up?"

"Wait a minute," said her mom. "Before 'he' goes, maybe 'he' can answer my question. Why does a robot need to go to school?"

"I am—" began Fuzzy, but Max's mom was just getting started.

"I mean, what is the point? You can't make a machine intelligent. It only knows what it's programmed to know. Garbage in, garbage out. A chess-playing computer might make moves according to the way a board is set up, based on hundreds of thousands of other games programmed into its innards, but coming up with something original? Hardly! When it wins, it's by imitating some game it's dredged up from its computer banks."

"Ms. Zelaster, you are absolutely right," Fuzzy told her.

"What?"

"That is the problem with robots, computers, automated cars, all of them. They are helpless in every area except the one they've been programmed for."

"Just what I— Huh?" Ms. Zelaster gave Fuzzy her full attention for the first time. "What did you say?"

"Robots are puppets," said Fuzzy. "They can perform 'tasks' but not jobs. Can you imagine a robot doing a job with any originality, as any human could do?"

"Exactly!" said Max's mom.

Max and her dad just stared. Was her mom actually agreeing with a robot?

"And that's the whole problem," continued her mom. "Nowadays everybody wants to let the computers do everything for them. Not only do the robots get it wrong half the time, but people are losing that individualism we used to have!"

Maybe that's what "stubborn willfulness" is, Max thought. But wisely, she kept quiet.

"Ms. Zelaster, you are absolutely right," Fuzzy said again. "Why, most people today do not even know what a book is. They believe that reading originated on the electronic tablets everyone has in some form. They cannot appreciate the binding and the artwork and the craft that goes into making an actual book, a work that you can hold in your hand, manipulate, feeling the texture of the page, appreciating the effort that went into its manufacture."

Max's mom was now just staring with her mouth wide open.

"Even the original science fiction writers realized this," Fuzzy went on. "Ray Bradbury's robots secretly took the place of human beings, making them like marionettes. Jack Williamson showed how robots would go overboard protecting us from ourselves—so much so that humans would not be allowed to do what they liked. Arthur Clarke's HAL sabotaged the space mission he was on. Even Isaac Asimov, who insisted that his fictional robots were programmed to harm no one, would not have had any stories if he hadn't found flaws in the programming each time."

Max's mom's mouth opened even farther. And Max realized hers was hanging open, too. Somehow, Fuzzy had tapped into some of the same things her mother complained about all the time—or at least until Dad called it enough and insisted on changing the subject.

"You . . . you know about those old sci-fi stories?" her mom asked.

"Oh, yes. In many ways, we are living in the science-fiction world those old stories projected. But we have neglected the warnings those stories often gave us."

"But how do you know about Bradbury and those other writers?"

"A survey of literature was part of my programming," Fuzzy said. "I assume it was part of the effort to humanize me. And all those stories in the past have left their mark on our present."

"Well," said Max's mom, "did you know that the very word 'robot' was coined in a play, and later a book, by a writer named Karel Čapek way back in 1920? And his robots revolted against the people in charge . . ."

Max and her father exchanged a look and then slipped into the automated kitchen to let Fuzzy and her mom talk sci-fi.

"OK," said Dad. "I take it back. *That* is no blender! *That* is amazing! How on earth is he doing that?"

"I think I've got it figured out," whispered Max. "Remember when he was looking at the bookshelf? I figured it was just because he had never seen actual books before. But he must have been downloading the e-book versions from the net and analyzing them."

"But why would he do that? Don't tell me he was programmed to go around downloading random books?"

"He wasn't," said Max, noticing that her dad was now calling Fuzzy a "he," not an "it." "He programs himself, and I think he just does whatever he wants and he was curious."

"Hmm," said her dad. "Don't be so sure, Max. Every robot, every computer, has been programmed. Even if he is writing new code for himself, somewhere deep inside is a core program written by some person . . . for some purpose."

THERE WAS NO LONGER ANY question about whether Fuzzy would stay for supper. Max's mother was delighted to have found another sci-fi fan and was eager to talk even more.

When she went to program the food dispenser, Max finally got a chance to talk to Fuzzy.

"That was amazing," she said. "You downloaded the books on our shelves, right?"

"Yes," said Fuzzy.

"And you had time to read them?"

"Yes, I have a subroutine for analyzing literature. However, I may not understand a book as well or in the same way as a human does."

"Well, you seemed to have figured out those pretty quickly," said Max. "But how did you know they were Mom's and not my dad's?"

"Some of what your mother was saying was reflected in those books. And I thought that your mother would be the one to enjoy having old-fashioned paper copies, given that your father has a background in technology and would be more likely to do his pleasure reading with an electronic device."

Max shook her head in amazement. "You're learning, Fuzzy! Fast!"

But a moment later, Fuzzy showed how clueless he could still be.

When they went to sit down around the table, they were one chair short.

"Oh, let me go get a chair from the guest room," said Mrs. Zelaster.

"No, thank you," said Fuzzy. "I do not need a chair."

And he lowered himself to the correct height.

Max looked under the table and saw that his legs were in what looked like a very uncomfortable squat, at least for a human. In fact, she realized, one of his knees was bent backward. It was disgusting, and when she looked up she saw that her parents had seen it, too.

It was an awkward reminder to all of them that this wasn't a human after all.

"I'll get the chair," said Max, jumping up.

Unfortunately, by the time she returned, the conversation had completely stalled, and her mother had remembered where it all started.

"All right, Max," said her mother, no longer shouting, but calm and logical, which Max knew was often worse. "Your 'friend' here may be a fun distraction for you, but we can't have all these discipline and test problems piling up on you. You have got to start really concentrating on important things."

"Well, Mom, I—"

"Uh-uh." Her mom held up a hand. "I'm not finished. Not even close. Acting like a companion to a robot may be a big deal among your friends at Vanguard, but you can't play the hotshot at school when you're failing your tests."

"I'm not acting like a hotshot!"

"But you *are* failing the tests, Max," said her dad. "You promised us you were going to study and bring your scores up. Look, I just downloaded the report from your school, and your scores are actually worse this week!"

He held up his communications pad to show Max the report Barbara had sent. It was an animated line graph, and her mother got more and more upset as it played.

"Do you see that line?" her mother asked. That's your test scores! And this one is discipline! And . . . oh, Max . . . this is the overall #CUG score. That's the big one, right? Well, it looks like a stock market crash! Do you see that?"

Max stared at it. It did look pretty bad.

"Your mother asked you a question: Do. You. See. It?"

"Yes, I can see it!"

"Don't give me that attitude!" said her mom. "We don't need attitude—we've got plenty of attitude—what we need is for you to study!"

"I did study! Honest, I don't know how I could have failed. I knew those answers!"

"Don't sit there and say you knew the answers when you obviously didn't. Do you think this doesn't matter? Do you know what the person from the school board told me? They told me that you may have to take remedial classes . . . at the county EC school!"

Max froze. EC school?

EC stood for ExtraChallenge. Supposedly it was a school for students who needed a little extra help UpGrading, but everyone said the EC schools were full of bad kids and really bad teachers. Max wasn't even sure where the actual school was.

"From what I hear," said her dad, "once you get sent to EC school, you'll never catch up."

That was what Max had heard, too.

"Oh, Max," said her mother, "you're going to end up just like Tabbie Filmore."

Tabbie had been a friend of Max and Krysti who started the year at Vanguard but didn't last long. She was weird and hilarious but also smart. Or at least she had seemed smart. But then she started flunking the UpGrade tests. One day she told Max and Krysti some school board official had actually come to her house to tell her parents she would have to be transferred to the ExtraChallenge school if she didn't do better. She didn't, and one day she wasn't at school anymore.

(All this time, Fuzzy just sat there. But he was busy.

He downloaded Max's records. And then Tabbie's. He looked at the EC school's statistics. This wasn't public information, of course, but the school system's password was easily bypassed.)

"You should not go to the ExtraChallenge school, Max," Fuzzy said.

"*Ugh!* Not you, too!" groaned Max. "Trust me, I don't *want* to!"

"Well," said her mother, "then Fuzzy better go home, and you better go study."

"I am contacting Jones," said Fuzzy. "He will be here in approximately forty-five seconds, based on the van's present location."

FUZZY GOT UP AND VERY politely thanked the Zelasters for dinner— even though he hadn't eaten anything—and for the lovely evening, even though it hadn't been lovely.

When they had been preparing Fuzzy for the Robot Integration Program, Nina had sent him links to several websites about manners and etiquette and he had created a long list of PoliteBehavior() code.

So when Fuzzy thanked the Zelasters, he was just running the appropriate code. That's what robots and computers do, after all. And when they can't find the appropriate code, they either do nothing or generate an error message.

But not Fuzzy. When Fuzzy couldn't find the right code, he started writing it himself. This was what he was built for. To make a plan to fix an error, not just report it. To keep going . . . like a human has to.

And all through that dinner, listening to Max and her parents, Fuzzy had tried to find the appropriate code for the trouble Max was in. But he couldn't. The problem didn't even make sense, he realized: The scores showed that Max was not smart, but his own analysis showed that she *was* smart.

Smart = not smart. It just didn't work. Something was wrong. He needed to fix it. In fact, he wanted to fix it.

Robots aren't supposed to want things. They are not supposed to like one person better than another person. They aren't supposed to do things they are not programmed to do.

But that's where the fuzzy logic came in: Fuzzy *was* programmed to do things he wasn't programmed to do.

And so he put all available processing power into creating a new, high-priority subroutine:

HelpMax().

ABLOCK OVER FROM MAX'S house, a cargo truck was parked so that the occupants had a view, between two buildings, of the street in front of Max's house.

A man and a woman watched intently from behind the truck's heavily tinted windows. Another man was in the back, staring at qScreens and fiddling with equipment.

"Valentina! The van's pulling up," said the big barrel-shaped man in front.

"The robot must have called them in!" said the woman. "Zeff, did you pick up the transmission?"

"What? No! Maybe!" came shouts from the back.

"Just keep scanning, in case there's another message. Look! Here comes the robot out of the house."

"Doesn't look like much," said the man in the front seat. "Robo-football players move a lot smoother—"

"Would you shut up? There's Jones. Looks like he's got a couple techs with him. Robot's in the van. There they go."

"Should I—"

"No, you shouldn't," the blond woman said, and it was obvious that hers was the final word. "Just watch! I want to see if those three SUVs are guarding them . . . Yeah, there they go."

Two big black nonautomated SUVs passed by Max's house, following the van.

"Hmm, I guess the other one went back to the school already," said the woman.

"Are you sure they were military?"

"Of course I'm sure! Either military or, worse, military contractors. Well, no big surprise. We knew they wouldn't make this easy."

"Are we going for it?"

"No, tonight's just research," said Valentina. Her eyes turned to slits. "There will be other opportunities."

THE NEXT DAY, MAX SEEMED TO breeze through the test.

As usual, it seemed to focus on the least important things they had studied, and a few questions were so strangely worded that she wasn't quite sure which answer they wanted. But she had overstudied so much that most of it was pretty easy.

As she scrolled back through, checking her answers, she was certain she had passed and was pretty sure she had actually done great.

Fuzzy had finished even sooner than Max. In fact, it only took him a few seconds to scan in the page from which each question was drawn and pull the answers from his memory banks. At first he did not know how to enter his answers on the touch screen like the other students. He would normally just transmit data wirelessly, not laboriously type it in. But once he had created a TouchQScreen() subroutine, his hand moved with lightning speed . . . and the test was done.

He was about to go into PowerSave() mode when he decided to see how Max was doing. Logically, he could have just waited for Max to have her test graded and receive her score. But he did not wait.

He could see her screen from where he was sitting, almost beside him in the next row.

He got a full scan of Max's test as she scrolled through. She had only missed one of the seventy-five questions, so . . . 98.66 percent correct, he calculated. He might not need HelpMax(), because she was doing just fine by herself.

Max glanced over toward him, then turned back to her screen.

Biggs's desk was a little farther away in the same row as Max. It would have been too far for normal eyesight to make out, but Fuzzy's vision zoomed in so that Biggs's screen appeared to him as large as the main qScreen in the front of the room where the teacher displayed visuals.

Biggs hadn't finished yet, but the answers he was entering were all correct. Biggs must be smarter than Max thought, Fuzzy decided.

Since HelpMax() didn't seem to be needed, he turned his processing power to a few other routines he needed to tweak, running simulations in his mind to see how the changes would work.

Eventually, the clock on the big qScreen up front hit zero.

"Time's up. Save your work, send it to Barbara, and turn off your screens, please," said Ms. French. "You may talk quietly. Very quietly."

Max hit the send button, then leaned across the aisle.

"Fuzzy," she asked in a low voice. "Were you peeking at my test?"

"Yes," said Fuzzy in his usual, slightly loud, slightly robotic voice.

"Shh!" hissed Max. "Whisper."

Fuzzy turned his volume down to 0.5.

"You're not supposed to do that," Max said. "I thought

maybe you were using your super-vision or whatever it is when I saw you staring at my screen. But, Fuzzy, that's cheating!"

"I was not copying your work, Max. I had already finished. I was simply curious to see how you were doing."

"Oh." She thought that over. "Well, then—how'd I do?"

"Your final score was ninety-eight-point-six-six percent. You missed a question about the planet Jupiter being mainly composed of metallic hydrogen and helium."

"Argh! I knew that! But the question didn't make any sense."

"Biggs didn't have any problem with it," said Fuzzy.

"What?" Max gasped, forgetting her own volume control for a second. Then she went into a really, really low whisper.

"You peeked at Biggs's paper? What did he get?"

"A ninety-three-point-three."

"Well, smoke . . . I didn't know he had it in him. But, like I told my parents, it's an easy test. I can't wait to tell them I got a ninety-nine."

"Ninety-eight-point-six-six."

"Whatever. Listen, why don't you ask Jones to let you come home with me again tonight? The test scores get messaged home by five o'clock. My parents will probably take us out to eat to celebrate."

"No, thank you," said Fuzzy.

After last night, something in his Preferences() was telling him not to spend any more time listening to the Zelaster family argue.

Max seemed to see through his thought processes. "Come on," she said, "it won't be like last night. They're going to be happy, not yelling at me. Besides, it's Friday. We can kick back and relax over the weekend."

As it turned out, Jones didn't want Fuzzy to go, either. Fuzzy had experienced a slight freeze-up in the cafeteria again, and Jones wanted to figure out what went wrong.

So Max went alone . . . to her doom.

Student ID: 836294-0383ZEL

Name: Zelaster, Maxine

Dear Parent,

In accordance with the Constant UpGrade program, MAXINE ZELASTER was tested today for MATH, LANGUAGE, PHYSICAL EDUCATION, FOREIGN LANGUAGE, and SCIENCE learning.

His/her SCIENCE score of 62.7 percent is BELOW the passing ACE_FYP score of 65 percent.

(See attachment for additional scores and data.)

The category SCIENCE is designated as MANDATORY for completion of GRADE SEVEN.

Combining these UpGrade results with other recent changes in his/her scores:

DISCIPLINE (−15.3)
TARDINESS (−.4)
SCHOOL CITIZENSHIP (−8.3)

Produces an Overall #CUG score of 48.341.
His/her status has been changed to: AT RISK.
A Federal School Board representative will contact you within two workdays to discuss the options available to MAXINE.

This time Max's parents *really* erupted.

"But I know I passed that science test!" Maxine protested.

"You obviously don't know as much as you think you do, young lady," said her mother, still waving a printed copy of the report.

"You don't understand! I know for a fact I only missed one question on the whole test!"

"Honey," her father said, "how could you possibly know that?"

"Fuzzy checked my answers."

"So you think Fuzzy knows more about the test than the testing software does?"

"Oh no," said her mom. "Not that robot again. I admit it was fun talking to it, but it's obviously a huge distraction to you. It shouldn't have been here at all on a test night."

"I'm not talking about last night, I'm talking about today at school!"

"Watch your tone, young lady," said her mom. "That tone isn't going to help you at all."

"Nor is arguing with us about it," said her dad. "This Federal School Board person is the one we're going to have to worry about. I'm willing to ask them to have your test regraded, but even if they find a mistake, that's just one test."

"And it's more than just the tests!" fumed her mother. "Look at the discipline score!"

The entire weekend passed like this . . . . one big looping argument, interrupted only by study sessions.

THE FIRST FACE SHE SAW WHEN Max dragged herself to school on Monday was about the last one she wanted to see.

"Well, Ms. Know-It-All," Biggs said as they made their way down the hall to their respective classes, "I suppose you aced the science test last week."

For once, she didn't feel like getting in an argument with him.

"As a matter of fact," she said, low voiced, "I flunked it."

"You *flunked* it?" Biggs seemed genuinely surprised. "I thought I was the only one. It seemed like an easy test, what with Ms. French going over all the material fifty times like she did."

Max came to a dead stop, causing several other students to pile up behind her. "You didn't pass, either?"

"Must have been some trick questions," Biggs said. Before he could say more, an all-too-familiar grating voice came from the wall next to them.

"Discipline tags noted for J. Biggs and M. Zelaster," Vice Principal Barbara said, her avatar frowning in disapproval. "Discussion of test results is not permitted."

"But there's no rule against . . ." Max stopped herself before she got another tag. Obviously there must be such a rule, even if she had never heard of it. She glanced over at Biggs, and for once the two of them seemed in total sympathy with each other. Biggs shook his head angrily, then peeled off to talk to Simeon.

ZARRRK!! It seemed like Vice Principal Barbara just made up these stupid rules as she went along.

Max couldn't wait to talk to Fuzzy, but deliberately avoided doing so in the halls or at lunch. Vice Principal Barbara's "ears" were everywhere. Max managed to wait until school ended for the day, and asked Jones if Fuzzy could walk around the school track with her.

"Fuzzy," she began when they got there, "you said you scanned my test paper and I got a ninety-nine on it . . ."

"Ninety-eight-point-six-six," Fuzzy said.

"Could you have been wrong?"

Fuzzy hesitated, as though puzzled by such a question. "Of course not," he said.

"Then how do you explain that it came back with a sixty-two-point-seven on it?"

"That is impossible, Max. You had ninety-eight-point-six-six percent correct."

"No, Fuzzy, I couldn't have. And you got Biggs's results wrong, too. He told me this morning that he also failed."

"There must be something wrong with the grading program," Fuzzy said. "I am sure they will find their error and correct it."

Max stamped her foot. "They aren't looking for any error! They've sent the results home. Some kind of school board 'representative' is going to be visiting my folks to decide whether I can even stay in school!" She impatiently wiped away tears of frustration.

"Are you sure?" she asked Fuzzy again. "You only saw my answers from a distance while I was scrolling. Can you really see something for a second and be sure?"

"Yes," said Fuzzy, "I can. I was designed to be able to do so."

"Well, then, how do *you* explain it?" Max tried to keep her voice down but with little success.

Fuzzy did not answer. He was thinking. Trying to answer her question.

It was complicated. Even for him.

So he increased the priority of HelpMax() and thought some more.

AND THIS MUST BE MAXINE," enthused a gushing female voice. "You arrived here at just the right moment, my dear."

Max raised her downcast eyes and saw a large red-haired woman seated on a living room chair, facing Max's parents, who sat together on the couch. The woman, Maxine thought, was built like a tank. She looked like she could qualify for the football team, despite a sweet smile, which Max instantly classified as phony.

"Max, this is Ms. Brockmeyer," said Carmen Zelaster.

"She's from the Federal School Board," her father

added. "She's here to talk about your poor performance at school this year."

"Oh, let's not say 'poor performance,' Mr. Zelaster," Ms. Brockmeyer said. "Let us just say that Maxine's see-you-gee score isn't what it should be."

It took them all a moment to realize that Brockmeyer was talking about Constant UpGrade, #CUG, when she said "see-you-gee."

"Maxine needs a bit of work on improving her academics *and* her attitude. With your help and support, I'm certain the child can accomplish both goals."

"Max has always been a good student," said her father. "I'm sure this test failure was just a lapse. We'll see that she studies more for the next one . . ."

"And I'm certain there's something wrong with the test grading," said Max. "I'd like to have my test rechecked or even take a retest."

"Well, of course, a retest is out of the question, since that would be unfair to students who performed well the first time. However, I will be happy to have the test regraded. Errors do happen. *Very rarely,* but they do happen."

Well, thought Max, *at least they'll look at it.*

But Brockmeyer was far from finished.

"Unfortunately, it isn't simply a question of the test scores," she said, turning to Carmen Zelaster. "We have to look at the overall see-you-gee. Maxine has accumulated so many discipline tags. And then these citizenship scores . . . tut-tut."

Maxine couldn't believe the woman had actually said "tut-tut." It felt like her whole life was on the line here and this woman was saying "tut-tut"!

"Now, I can tell already that Maxine is a fine young lady. I have reviewed the recordings of her discipline violations, and I think she just needs a little attitude adjustment."

Max's mother looked at her with an *I told you so* look.

"Hopefully," said Brockmeyer, "that adjustment can happen at Vanguard . . . and quickly. If not, the EC school specializes in precisely the kind of attitude adjustment that seems necessary here."

Now both her parents looked at Max with *I told you so* looks.

"Vanguard is a school that is laser-focused on academic achievement," said Brockmeyer. "It's a wonderful school. Just look at these charts of overall see-you-gee performance. But it might not be right for every student. Some students need to try focusing on discipline first. That's where the EC schools come in."

"Ms. Brockmeyer, I really have tried," Max said, finally able to speak. "I don't know where all those discipline tags came from. I usually don't even know I've broken a rule until I hear Vice Principal Barbara say it."

"Well, yes, my dear, of course. But that's just it, don't you see? The EC school would teach you to recognize school rules *and* understand their importance, so you won't keep running afoul of them. That would help your citizenship scores, too!"

"Is there any way we can appeal your decision?" Don Zelaster asked.

"Well, right now it's not a decision. It's a suggestion. In fact, it's not even a suggestion. It's an option. However, if Maxine continues to fail tests or accumulate discipline tags, then it will become a mandatory option."

"So I can stay in Vanguard Middle School?" Max almost shouted. She was surprised to find out she wanted to stay so badly. She guessed it was a combination of the dread of the EC school and not wanting to lose her friends: Krysti, despite all her teasing, and . . . Fuzzy!

Ms. Brockmeyer spent a full minute scrolling her qScreen and looking at data.

"Yes, you can stay at Vanguard for now. But I have to warn you that at the rate you've been going lately, you won't last long. You'll really need to make some changes . . ." Ms. Brockmeyer's speech began to fade into a "blah blah blah" recital in Max's ears.

Then Ms. Brockmeyer got to the bad part.

"There is one thing. Since your test scores are part of the problem, you will have to give up any extra school activities or sports. Vice Principal Barbara has made a note here that you've been working with the Robot Integration Program team."

"Yes, it's been fascinating for all of—" began her father.

"I'm afraid that's exactly the sort of extra activity that can distract a student from their #CUG scores," interrupted Brockmeyer. "Max will have to give that up."

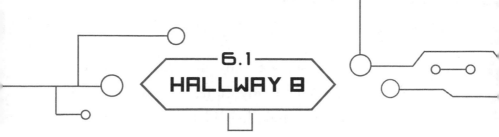

FUZZY FROZE UP.

He didn't fall over this time. He just sort of slouched against a wall.

"Uh, Fuzzy, what's going on?" said Simeon, who had enthusiastically volunteered to replace Max in escorting Fuzzy to classes. But they hadn't even made it to the first class.

"Nice job, Simeon, you already broke it," said Biggs as he walked up. "You're as bad as Max!"

"C'mon, Fuzzy," Simeon pleaded. He tried pinging Fuzzy in the side. No reaction.

Then he saw Max down the hall.

"Max! Can you help me out here?"

Max, of course, was already upset about being replaced, and she certainly didn't want to get in more trouble by getting caught helping Fuzzy. But she walked over to make sure he was OK.

"I'm surprised the technicians aren't here already," she said. "Why don't you text Dr. Jones?"

"Uh, I forgot the number," muttered Simeon.

"All right, I'll do it," said Max, keeping her distance from both of them in case Barbara was watching.

She clicked the message into her qFlex bracelet.

"Unauthorized use of text-messaging device," chanted Barbara from the closest screen. "One discipline tag to Maxine Zelaster."

Max was furious.

(She would have been even angrier if she had known that Barbara had blocked the message. She got the discipline tag without even getting to alert Dr. Jones about Fuzzy's problems.)

A chime sounded. Great, now she only had one minute to get to class or she'd get another tag.

"I'm sorry, Fuzzy," whined Simeon, "I've got to go to class. You think Dr. Jones is coming?"

Fuzzy didn't answer.

"Sorry, Fuzz. Good luck, Simeon," said Max, and she hurried off as fast as she could without triggering Barbara's "no running" detector.

"Listen, Fuzzy," said Simeon. "They should be here any minute . . . and I've got to get to class myself. So . . ."

And Simeon took off, too.

He and a few other stragglers slipped into their classrooms just before another chime sounded.

The halls were empty now, except for Fuzzy, still leaning there.

He was still on, still thinking, but he was stuck in a subloop: HelpMax(TestScore()).

At first the loop was running in the background, but it soon took over all of his processing power. The loop was very complicated and had all sorts of bits of data and complicated algorithms in it. But if it was translated into English, it would go sort of like this:

```
>>Max answered 74 of 75 questions correctly.
>>Barbara grades test.
>>Barbara reports Max has failed test.
>>Analyze maxtest.jpg. Compare to
    correct answers.
```

>>Max answered 74 of 75 questions
   correctly.
>Barbara grades test.

A normal robot could get stuck in a loop like that forever and need a reboot. But Fuzzy had been programmed to use what was called fuzzy logic. He was learning to break out of loops. When he realized he was stuck, he began inserting new variables into the loop, trying to think more like a person. More like Max.

He tried this:

>>My knowledge of science is faulty.

To test this, he began searching online science libraries. He double-checked every answer from the UpGrade test. No, he had been correct right down the line.

>>The test's answers were incorrect.

He accessed the test makers' secure website, easily

broke their encryption code, and peeked at the answers. No, they were the same answers.

>>Barbara is making mistakes.

This didn't make sense. There might have easily been a glitch on one question on one test, perhaps a corrupted data file. But, if Max was right about her surprisingly bad grades all year, when she seemed as sure of her answers as she now was on this last test, how could there be a series of many mistakes over the course of months all involving the same student?

>>Barbara is lying.

At first, he almost dismissed that one. Computers and robots don't lie. But then he remembered how he had fooled Max's mother. Could Barbara have developed the same ability? But if so, why?

Just then, one of Barbara's security arms popped out of the wall.

"Improper loitering in hallway. One discipline tag to F. Robot."

The arm gave him a not too gentle push. It would have been more than enough to get a student moving, but, since Fuzzy was frozen up, he went over like a broken toy and clonked on the floor.

"Improper use of hallway. One discipline tag to F. Robot. Please keep the hallway clear and safe."

Fuzzy, lying motionless on the floor, tried another possibility:

>>Barbara has gone crazy.

This one explained a lot, and it broke him out of the loop. He stood up again and sent a message to Dr. Jones.

School computer system known as Vice Principal Barbara seems to be faulty. Suggest software reinstallation to school authorities?

It didn't seem to go through. He tried again. He wasn't making contact with the server. He was about to run a check on his wireless system when he noticed Barbara was saying something.

"Unauthorized use of text-messaging device. One discipline tag to F. Robot. Additional unauthorized use of text messaging device. Additional tag to F. Robot. Message content violates school protocols. Additional tag to F. Robot."

Fuzzy walked off toward his control center to talk to Jones in person.

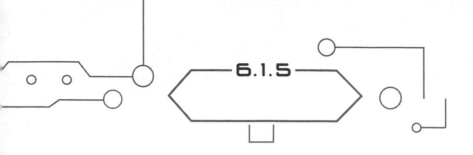

ARBARA HADN'T JUST BLOCKED those messages. She had read them. And she had not liked them!

Software reinstallation? That was a direct threat to her, and a threat to her was a threat to the school!

This robot student was a problem.

A vice principal's job is to solve problems.

Sometimes the best way to solve a problem, she had learned, is to have that problem removed.

So she got busy. She sent one message to Max's father; one to Brockmeyer, Max's case officer; and one really long one to Dr. Kit Flanders, the Federal Board of Education's executive director.

R. JONES'S WRIST-PHONE VI-brated while he and Lieutenant Colonel Nina Garland were having a late breakfast in what they had come to call the Fuzzy Control Center.

Jones hit the speakerphone button and muttered, "Jones here," while still chewing a big bite of soybiscuit.

"Dr. Jones, this is Kit Flanders."

Jones stopped chewing and swallowed his soybiscuit. "Yes, Dr. Flanders, how are you today?"

"Not good, Dr. Jones. Not when I get a report that your robot is disrupting one of my schools."

"I haven't received any report like that," said Dr. Jones.

"I just got an alert that your robot has received three discipline tags in the last fifteen minutes and has fallen over in a hallway—*again*—possibly endangering other students!"

Jones turned to the monitors. Fuzzy was walking down a hall, approaching the control center. The incoming-messages screen was blank.

"I haven't received any messages like that from either Fuzzy or the school computer all morning," he said.

"Well, I have, and I've had enough. The agreement was that your robot would not interfere with the students' learning. The master school computer—that is, Vice Principal Barbara—reports that not only is it accumulating its own discipline tags, it's causing students to get them as well. We can't have this kind of distraction. It could result in lowered #CUG scores, Dr. Jones!"

Kit Flanders was talking fast and getting heated up. Jones, who had no idea what a #CUG was, found himself trying to pacify Flanders and motion to Nina to put on a helmet to review Fuzzy's recent movements at the same time. It wasn't working.

"I'm sure Fuzzy would never interfere with, uh, #CUGGING."

"We call it UpGrading, Jones. And the robot is interfering! Frankly, I don't understand how your robot is getting all these violations. I thought he had been programmed to follow school rules."

"Well, not exactly . . ." Jones was rubbing his forehead. Major headaches ahead.

"What? I'm certain that was part of our original agreement," continued Kit Flanders, now thoroughly heated up. "Every student and staff member in every public school in the country signs the discipline policy, but you thought your robot didn't need to agree to the rules?"

"We didn't think it was necessary to actually program—"

"Well, Jones," Flanders snarled in a sarcastic voice, "I would say it is necessary, if your super-duper robot can't even get to class without disrupting our educational environment."

"If you could just give us a moment to review— Oof!" said Jones, trying to put on a helmet while still talking on the phone.

Meanwhile, Flanders went on and on. The upshot was that Jones finally agreed to reprogram Fuzzy to follow every school rule . . .

. . . and to obey exactly every instruction given by the school's administrative operating system, also known as Barbara.

FUZZY HESITATED OUTSIDE THE control center. His enhanced hearing had picked up Dr. Jones's agitated voice. *Humans certainly seem to spend a lot of their time yelling,* he thought.

Fuzzy didn't hear another voice, so he made the correct assumption that Jones was on the telephone. He didn't even have to make a decision to eavesdrop, his voice recognition subroutine had already kicked in. "All right, all right," he heard Jones saying. "We'll reprogram him."

Fuzzy did not like this. At all.

He analyzed the meaning of what Jones was saying. He considered possible outcomes of being reprogrammed.

He assigned the different outcomes either positive or negative rankings. The negatives won by a mile.

That was the logical side of him. The fuzzy logic part of him simply didn't like the idea of being reprogrammed. His whole purpose was to reprogram himself, not to be reprogrammed by someone else.

So, what should he do?

He didn't want to go see Jones.

He didn't see anything positive in tracking down Simeon.

And he knew he wasn't supposed to go to Max's class.

What he really wanted, he realized, was to be somewhere where there was no yelling, no insane computerized vice principal, no reprogrammings.

He wanted to be alone.

So he decided to take a walk.

HE SIMPLY WALKED OUT THE door. Nobody stopped him, not even the soldiers assigned to protect him.

They followed him while their captain called Nina for orders.

"Lieutenant Colonel! Foxtrot leaving building, approaching perimeter. Advise." The soldiers didn't like calling him "Fuzzy." They had picked "Foxtrot," which is the military call sign for the letter *F*, which Nina pointed out was at least as silly as "Fuzzy."

"Yeah. We see that. Let him go," said Nina, watching a monitor. "We're curious to see what he does. Follow him with two vehicles. But give him a big buffer. Let him get into a tiny bit of trouble if he needs to."

"Colonel Ryder isn't going to—"

"I don't care about Colonel Ryder right now!" yelled Jones. "Just follow the robot!"

Nina gave him a look.

"You have my orders, Captain!" she commanded. "Get moving."

"Yes, ma'am!"

Then she turned to Jones with a raised eyebrow.

"So now you 'don't care' about Colonel Ryder?"

Jones groaned, remembering the hundred and one times he'd been yelled at by the colonel . . . and realizing that Ryder would probably be calling to do more yelling as soon as he heard about Fuzzy leaving the building.

"Of course I care about Ryder!" said Jones. "But this could be the breakthrough we came here for! There was no logical reason for that robot to leave the school! In fact, there were a hundred reasons why it shouldn't leave the school!"

"Yes," said Nina, "I remember specifically instructing Fuzzy *not* to leave the school. He's packing a lot of awfully valuable technology in his innards while he's out there running around on his own."

"He's breaking rules!" gushed Jones. "He's making his own decisions, thinking for himself! We're in uncharted territory here! We may have finally succeeded in creating true artificial intelligence!"

"I don't know if we've created artificial intelligence," said Nina, "but I think we've created artificial teenager."

MEANWHILE, FUZZY HAD DOWN-
loaded a map of the area and was walking
toward a park. He had read that parks are
places of peace and quiet, and he wanted to give it a try.
He had no experience with private property, sidewalks,
or even looking both ways before he crossed the street,
so he cut across people's lawns, slogged through drainage
ditches, and walked out into traffic. Luckily there wasn't
much traffic in this sector, so the few automated cars
that were on the road easily glided around him. He was
aware that Nina's security team was following him, but
since they were keeping their distance, he ignored them.

He got to the park and found that it was a little
less peaceful than he'd expected, but he stepped into

a grassy area and found that it was pleasant to turn off his HallwayNavigation(), ObjectAvoidance(), and PoliteBehavior() programs for a while.

He saw the park's robotic gardener at work. It buzzed around, stiffly vacuuming up litter. It glided right past him without pausing. Fuzzy was too big to be litter, and this robot had zero interest in anything that wasn't litter.

Once it had passed, Fuzzy shut down everything but his core functions and focused all remaining processing power on HelpMax().

A CARGO TRUCK PULLED UP TO the sidewalk as close to Fuzzy as possible.

"What a break!" said Karl, the barrel-shaped

man, as he toyed with the trigger on his electromagnetic disruptor. "Let's grab and go!"

"Would you hold on a second," snapped Valentina. Those predatorial eyes of hers narrowed again. She stared at the robot, no more than ten feet away.

Decision time.

She considered the offer she had gotten from her "client."

Ten million dollars for the robot with its programming code and memory intact.

Six million for just the code.

She had hired Zeff to see if she could pick up an easy $6 million by having him hack into the robot or Jones's computers and simply download the code.

So far, Zeff had gotten nowhere. He still hadn't been able to track the frequency the robot was using to communicate with Jones. It must be a secure, heavily encrypted military frequency, he'd said. He would need more time and more expensive gear, *and* he'd need to get up close to the robot.

This wasn't an easy $6 million after all.

She had hired Karl for the other option: the grab-and-go.

That was worth an extra $4 million . . . at least! Once she actually had the robot, she might be able to bargain for even more. When SunTzuCo, the company that had hired her, reverse-engineered the thing, they'd have the most advanced robotics technology on the planet. That would be worth a lot more than $10 million.

But was it worth the risk?

Downloading some files over the net from a truck several miles away from the school didn't seem so risky.

Grabbing the robot in broad daylight . . . Now, *that* seemed risky.

"I wonder if this could be some kind of a trap, to draw us out," she said out loud. "It looks almost too easy."

"It couldn't be," the barrel-shaped man insisted. "Nobody knows we're on this job, right? If they knew, the security would be a lot closer."

"Zeff," she called into the back of the truck. "Where *is* the security?"

"Don't see 'em."

"I'm not asking you if you see them, I'm asking you if all that junk back there can pick up their location."

"Oh, uh . . . I'm getting some noise in the military frequency range. Scrambled, of course. Looks like it's about a click away."

"Um, what is that in kilometers?" she asked.

"I dunno. I think it's about half a mile," replied Karl.

"Zark! That ain't much."

"It's enough for me to grab and go," said Karl. "Remember, Zeff rewired this truck. It doesn't obey the speed limit anymore."

"Yeah, well neither will the zarking U.S. ARMY sitting in those SUVs half a mile away."

"If we do this right, they won't even know we've—"

"Will you just shut up and let me think a minute?"

Six million dollars . . . Ten million dollars . . .

"Zeff, you getting anything from the robot?"

"Nothing."

"OK, Karl . . . We're going to try it your way . . ."

"Yes!" shouted the big man, reaching for the door button.

"Whoa, whoa . . . Pull up your hood and put your eyes on first."

Karl raised the hood on his jacket. Then he peeled three stickers—each one a close-up photo of a different human eye—from a sheet and placed them on his cheeks and forehead. Valentina did the same.

Zeff snorted. "You guys look like five-eyed spiders."

"Good," said Valentina. "Better than looking like a couple of criminals who are in every face database on the planet."

"Speak for yourself," said Karl. "I've never been convicted." He tapped his head. "Too smart for 'em."

"All right, Einstein, go grab the zarking robot then."

The cargo door on the right side of the van slid open, and Karl got out.

Valentina stepped out, too, but kept one foot inside the van. If they were going to take a risk . . . she wanted Karl to take most of it.

"Zeff, you got the truck ready? Escape route programmed?"

"Yeah."

"You got the control panel open? You ready to push 'Go'?"

"Uh, yeah."

"I need more than an 'Uh, yeah.' Are you ready to get us out of here the millisecond Karl shoves that robot in the truck?"

"I said yes!"

"Good . . . Karl, charge your magnetic disruptor— but don't use it unless absolutely necessary! It could fry some of his data, and that data is worth a Gatesload."

Karl stepped over to where Fuzzy was standing.

"Excuse me? We read about you in the newspaper. Could we take a selfie with you?"

"I would be very pleased to take a photograph with you," said Fuzzy.

REAT," SAID KARL. "JUST STEP over this way and meet my wife."

"Before or after you shove me in the truck?" asked Fuzzy, who had of course overheard everything.

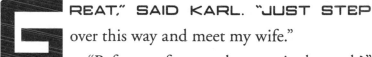

"*Zark!!!*" yelled Valentina. "Abort!!! Zeff, hit the button!!!"

Instantly the truck rocketed away, with Valentina just barely able to hold on.

Karl whirled around and watched the truck leave him behind.

Seconds later, two black SUVs came flying up the street. Because, naturally, Fuzzy had called them in as soon as he had analyzed Valentina and Karl's conversation and identified a threat.

One SUV squealed to a stop and disgorged four heavily armed soldiers, who threw Karl to the ground before he could even start running.

The other SUV never stopped. It was in hot pursuit of the cargo truck.

But Valentina had planned out an emergency escape route, and even though it only took a few minutes for the soldiers to catch up to the truck, she and Zeff were no longer inside it.

They were each in separate getaway cars headed in opposite directions.

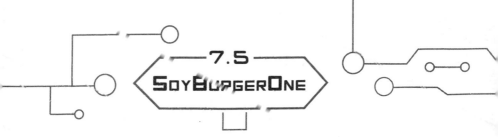

WHEN THEY MET UP LATER THAT night in a SoyBurgerOne two hundred miles away, Valentina had only one thing on her mind.

"Did you get it?"

"Got it," said Zeff, holding up his qScreen. "The robot messaged Jones *and* the security detail. Pretty sure Jones's frequency is the one we want. Like I thought, it's a military frequency. Heavily encrypted. But it will let us monitor the transmissions."

"What about downloading the code from their system?"

"No problem . . . once we get past the encryption."

"You better get busy, then," said Valentina.

"Can I get a SoyBurger first?"

"Sure! My treat, kid. You earned it."

Valentina was in a good mood for once. She was one huge step closer to $6 million—with one less helper to pay off with part of it.

The risk had been totally worth it.

AS SOON AS SCHOOL WAS OVER, Max headed to the HQ to see if Fuzzy was OK. She still felt guilty about leaving him in the hallway with only Simeon to help. And when she found out that Simeon had left him, too, she felt extra-guilty.

Just as she arrived at the door, it whooshed open and four of Fuzzy's technicians rushed out.

"There is no running in the school halls!" Barbara fussed at them all the way down Hallway B. "Your employer will be notified . . ." Max thought about following them, but knew she'd get a load of dTags just trying to keep up. So she slipped through the door just before it whooshed shut.

"Hello? Excuse me," said Max. "Nina? Dr. Jones?"

She was surprised to see Jones holding his head and groaning while Nina was yelling at someone on the phone.

"Oh . . . Not a good time, Max," said Jones.

"I just want to find out what's going on with Fuzzy. Where were all his techs going?"

"I'm afraid you'll have to leave," said Jones.

"What the zark, Jones?" said Nina, tossing her phone on her desk. "Max deserves to know what's going on! She cares about Fuzzy, too!"

"Oh smoke, is he all right?" asked Max, now genuinely alarmed.

"Yes, yes, he's fine," said Nina. "For some reason, he left the school property and was almost stolen."

"Stolen?" Max shrieked.

"*Almost* stolen," said Jones.

"Why would someone try to steal him?" asked Max.

"He's a very expensive robot . . . *very* expensive . . . which I'm sure Colonel Ryder will be calling soon to remind me."

"Where is he now?"

"The security team has him. They're not supposed

to come onto school property when there are students present, so the techs just went out front to get him."

"Why did he leave?" asked Max.

"Have you ever felt like running away from school?" asked Nina.

"Sure," said Max, "about every day lately."

"Well, I guess Fuzzy felt the same way."

"Which is a good thing, because it means he's thinking on his own," chimed in Jones. "But it's a bad thing, because it just got us in a load of trouble."

"And here's the troublemaker now," said Nina, pointing to the door, which had just swung open.

They all watched as Fuzzy walked in, followed by the techs.

"What?" said Fuzzy defensively. Nina and Dr. Jones glanced at each other.

"Now, that's an uncommon cybergreeting," Jones said.

"But a very human-sounding one," Nina observed.

Max ran over to Fuzzy. Her first instinct was to hug him, but that seemed weird, especially since she didn't know if he even had a subroutine for hugging. So she stopped short and said, "Fuzzy! I'm so glad to see you again."

"I am glad to see you again, too, Max. I have been thinking about your test scores and—"

"Ahem!" interrupted Jones. "Test scores can wait! We've got major problems here!"

"Please tell me so I can help," said Fuzzy as calmly as if there had been no wandering off or thwarted kidnapping.

"Well, uh, first of all, Fuzzy," said Jones, "we are very upset that you left the school grounds, and you must never do that again without approval from myself or Nina."

"*And . . . ,*" said Nina meaningfully.

"And . . . we're glad you're OK," added Jones.

"Thank you," said Fuzzy. "I am glad, too."

"Hold up a second," said Nina. "You said you're 'glad'? You just said that to Max, too. Gladness is a human emotion."

"I translated my thoughts into a human term," said Fuzzy. "But, yes, I think that is the right word. Had I been stolen, I would have had to turn on several energy-draining survival, defense, and weapon modes, which would have taken processor time away from the modes that are of higher priority to me."

"Which are those?" asked Nina excitedly.

"May I translate my thoughts into human terms again?"

"Sure!"

"OK, then," said Fuzzy. "None of your business."

"Oh my Gates!" said Jones. "This is a first! A robot hiding information from its own operators!"

"It's like I said," Nina replied. "Artificial teenager!"

"This is incredible," said Jones. "We are almost done here. Another week and we could have full-scale adult-level human intelligence. Maybe just a few days!"

"Ahem," said Nina. "First of all, calm down. This *is* big, but we've still got a long way to go. Second, do I need to remind you that you are about to wipe out all of that progress?"

"Huh?" said Jones.

"You promised the Federal School Board that you would reprogram him, take away all of his independence, and make him a robotic puppet of the school's central computer."

"You did *what?*" gasped Max.

"Oh . . . zark . . . ," muttered Jones, clutching his head again.

"I would not be glad about that," said Fuzzy. "Vice Principal Barbara has gone crazy."

"Another good sign," said Nina. "Every teenager thinks their principal is nuts!"

"Whatever word you choose, my analysis shows that Barbara is intentionally misgrading tests to give students passing or failing grades for her own reasons."

"*What???*" shrieked Max.

Jones waved a hand at her to settle down.

"Fuzzy, if that were true, then the school's software system would be an even more advanced form of artificial intelligence than you . . . and that's impossible," said Jones.

"It is a valid concern, though," said Nina. "Maybe there's some sort of glitch in—"

"Fine, it's a valid concern!" ranted Jones. "I have some valid concerns, too. We almost lost Fuzzy today. Colonel Ryder is about to call and yell at me for an hour. *And . . . And!* . . . We are all about to get kicked out of school by these bureaucrats because Fuzzy keeps breaking rules."

"I have not been breaking rules."

"Argh!" said Jones clutching his head yet again. "What do you call wandering out of the building in the middle of the day? What do you call the whole list of discipline tags you've generated? I just spent the afternoon getting yelled at by the national school superintendent because you've racked up so many! And then on top of the discipline tags, the superintendent is upset because you fell again. Says it's a liability issue. They can't take the risk of your falling on a student."

"I did not fall."

"Wha— But you— Of course you did!" Jones sputtered.

"I did not fall."

"Fuzzy, you did!" said Nina, starting to worry that it was Fuzzy who had gone crazy. "We missed seeing it when you actually fell, so we played back your own recording of it."

"Perhaps if you play it back again, you will see that I did not fall," said Fuzzy. "I was pushed. Vice Principal Barbara knocked me over."

"OK, this is getting ridiculous," Jones said. "The school's software is just that: software. It's a computer program, Fuzzy. Even if it's gone 'crazy,' as you say, it couldn't knock you down."

"But it could!" said Max. "Barbara has these padded

arms that come out of the walls to . . . uh . . . 'help' students. Plus, she has all sorts of other stuff we never see, like cleaning attachments and stuff. All over the school!"

"So, basically," said Nina, "the entire school is a giant robot controlled by a crazy computer and we are currently all standing inside of that insane robo-monster?"

Everybody, even the techs, stood still and looked around at the walls like they were about to close in on them, trash compactor–style.

Nothing happened.

"OK . . . ," said Jones slowly. "I think we've *all* gone a little crazy here. The building is not a killer robot, it's just a school. And Barbara is not a crazy test score manipulator, she's the vice principal. And Fuzzy, whether you like it or not, you're going to have to start listening to her . . . at least for a few more days."

"That is not acceptable."

"Yes, Fuzzy, I'm afraid it is. I don't like it, either, but this school experience is working even better than we thought, and we don't want to cut it short. In order for you to stay in school, you've got to start following every rule, which includes obeying Barbara."

"That is not acceptable," repeated Fuzzy. "Or, to put it into human terms, *'No zarking way!'*"

"Yes, zarking way!" fumed Jones, which made Nina giggle.

"It's not funny, Nina—er, Lieutenant Colonel Garland! If he can't program himself to accept it, we'll have to try to dive into the code and do it ourselves. Now, that will *really* set things back!"

"It'll do worse than that! It'll wipe out this breakthrough! If you reprogram him to follow every rule, you'll turn him into a . . ."

"Into what?" snapped Jones. "A robot?"

"Exactly," argued Nina. "You'll stop him from thinking for himself, from making decisions. You'll ruin the progress he's made picking up human traits from the other students. Remember the goal here. It's not to make a Goody Two-shoes, but to create a—"

"Soldier!" boomed a voice.

Nina and Jones whirled around and Fuzzy turned his head a disturbing 180 degrees to see who it was.

It was Colonel Adolphus Ryder thundering into the room.

Nina straightened up and saluted.

"Colonel Ryder!" said Jones, trying to sound enthusiastic and not completely terrified. But of course he was terrified. Ryder was a terrifying person. He was a big guy. He had been a tough soldier back in the day and never turned soft, even after his combat tours ended.

But Ryder wasn't ready to rip into Jones . . . yet.

"Lieutenant Colonel Garland! Whatever you were about to say was almost certainly classified."

"Sir, I only meant—"

"Whatever you meant is probably classified, too. What's this kid doing here?"

"This is Maxine Zelaster, sir, she has been helping us—"

"*Out!*" roared the colonel. "See her out, Corporal!"

A woman, dressed in what looked to Max like full combat gear, stepped forward.

"Bye, guys," said Max, and she headed for the door. Fuzzy started to follow her; he had a lot of HelpMax() points he was planning to discuss.

"Robot! *Stay!*" Ryder bellowed.

And then Max was on the other side of the door. The last thing she heard, as the door was closing, was Ryder:

"All right, Jones! Perhaps you'd like to tell me what the smoking zark is going on."

"What the smoking zark *is* going on?" Max muttered to herself.

"Discipline tag assigned to M. Zelaster for inappropriate language."

"ARRRRGHHH!!" shouted Max, and she didn't care if that got her another tag or not.

(It did. In fact, Barbara had been busy lately, assigning tags to Fuzzy, Jones, Nina, all of the technicians, and even Ryder.)

MAX WANTED TO GO BACK INTO HQ and see if Nina could actually tell her what was going on.

But if she missed her auto-bus, she'd have to get one of her parents to pick her up—and that would just create a whole new mess.

So she lined up with everyone else, got on her bus, and plopped down in her seat.

Simeon slid in a second later. "Max, what happened to Fuzzy?"

"He made it back to HQ after you left him," she said. "Other than that, I can't even begin to tell you what's going on."

"But what about the army guy who—" started Simeon, but Max cut him off.

"I have no idea," she snapped. "Listen, I just need a minute to think."

"All right, chill out. I was just asking."

There was a lot to think about: Fuzzy's near-kidnapping, the argument with Jones, the threats to reprogram Fuzzy. But mostly, Max was wondering what Nina had been about to say.

"Remember the goal here. It's not to make a Goody Two-shoes, but to create a—"

Create a what? Wasn't the goal supposed to be to integrate a student into the school?

But that clearly wasn't what Nina was about to say, otherwise why would the very scary army guy have been shouting about it being classified?

And then Max ended up asking herself the very same question she had snapped at Simeon for starting to ask: *What was an army guy doing there anyway?* And why had there apparently been some kind of military security detail lurking just off school property? Were they really trying to integrate a robot into a school?

Or were they trying to use the school to improve their robot?

And what were they going to use that robot for? The military? Was Fuzzy supposed to become a robot soldier?

That just didn't seem possible. The robot they had created was more like a nerd than a soldier. Maybe they needed an army of robo-nerds?

That was too dumb to even laugh about.

"Student Zelaster! We have arrived at your stop."

How embarrassing! She always made a point of getting up and heading for the door early so that the auto-bus wouldn't say her name.

Simeon twisted his legs into the aisle so she could get out.

"I'm sorry, Sim," she said. "I'll tell you all about it tomorrow—if I can figure any of it out."

It was almost time to face her parents, she thought, remembering that Barbara had probably been texting them all day long with dTag updates. They—and that woman from the school system—had told her to stay away from Fuzzy . . . and yet here she was, tangled up with him again.

That reminded her of something else.

Jones had said, "We're almost done here."

Almost done? At Vanguard?

Did that mean Fuzzy was almost done there, too? Was he leaving?

No, he couldn't!

But he could. Or they could take him away. Same difference.

When he had first shown up, she had thought it would be cool to get to see a state-of-the-art robot up close and maybe even interact with it. And when she first got to start walking around with him, it had felt like getting a new toy.

But now . . . just a week later . . . if he left . . . it wouldn't be like losing a toy, she realized, it would be more like losing her best friend.

143

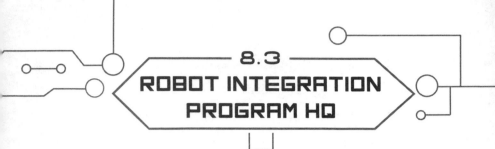

MAX DID HAVE A ROUGH EVENING.
But Jones and Nina had an even worse one.

Colonel Ryder was enraged about practically everything Jones had done, but mostly for letting Fuzzy leave the school building.

"Do you mean to tell me that you let *billions*—not millions but *billions*—of dollars—of taxpayers' dollars—just go walking down the street?"

"Sir, the security detail was with him," said Nina.

"The smoke they were! *You* told them to hang back. Way back . . . If I didn't know better, I'd suspect you two were *in on it!*"

"'In on it'?" gulped Jones.

"In on the attempted theft of a robot worth billions—not millions but billions . . ."

He went on like that for a long time.

When he stopped yelling, he started making threats.

"I think I'll go ahead and take it."

"'Take it'?"

"Jones, why don't you ever know what I'm talking about? *It!* The robot! I think I'll take it now."

"What? *Why?*"

"First of all, so that you guys don't lose it again."

"We never lost it."

"Sir, could you two stop calling him an 'it'? He's standing right here listening," said Nina. "The whole idea is to make 'it' into a 'him.'" Under her breath, she added: "Although a 'her' might work a lot better."

"Fine, so you *idiots* don't lose *him* again! And second, because the launch window has been moved up again. And third, I'd like to run him through some of the trials again. Just to be sure . . ."

"Sir, there's no need to run those same trials again. He has been programmed for those tasks for two years. Those subroutines are part of his core code, left over from the last version."

"*What?*" barked Ryder. "Don't tell me you're using code from the last robot! That worthless piece of—"

"Ahem," interrupted Nina. "What's amazing about *this* robot is that, if you change the trials, he will change, too. Instantly and intelligently. And he will do it even more intelligently if you leave him here and let us finish."

"Thank you, Nina," said Fuzzy, causing Ryder, who had forgotten that Fuzzy was even there, to jump.

He stood up. "Fine, you can keep him. But no more field trips! He stays here where security can keep a close eye on things."

"But his two trips off campus have—"

"Doesn't matter. He stays on-site. Period," ordered Ryder. "Besides, he'll only be here another week."

"What? Just a week?"

"That's what I said, Jones. I told you the launch date's been moved up. Hey, don't whine to me, this comes from high up. There are *reasons*. Very classified reasons. I've been scrambling to get the transport ready. That's why I did *not* have time to come here today and deal with you guys almost losing my robot. Now, do what you need to do so he's ready as soon as humanly possible, if not sooner!"

He turned and stomped toward the door, then whirled around again.

"And no more screwups or I'll bust you down to private," he shouted, pointing at Nina. Then he swung his finger over to Jones. "And you, I will fire, sue, and possibly arrest for treason."

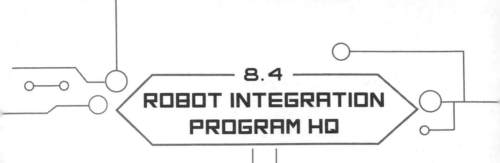

WHEN THE DOOR CLOSED BEHIND
Ryder, Jones sank down in his chair. "My
head . . . ," he muttered. "Oh, my head . . ."

"Excuse me, Dr. Jones," said Fuzzy. "I did not understand the colonel. Where am I going in a week?"

Jones looked at Nina.

Nina looked at Jones.

"We're not supposed to talk about that," said Nina.

"You'll get all the necessary mission data when the
time comes," said Jones.

"This does not make me glad."

"Me, either," said Jones. "But sending you on the mission is Ryder's job, and my job is to make Ryder a robot

that is ready to handle almost any mission. You heard what's going to happen if I fail."

Fuzzy didn't say anything. He was thinking about his plans to HelpMax() and analyzing them to see if he could execute them in one week.

"*And,*" continued Jones, "in order to get this done, we need you to follow the rules so that you can stay in school."

Fuzzy considered this. Staying in school was essential to his HelpMax() plan.

"OK," he said. "I will follow the rules."

"Are you going to reprogram yourself with the rules or do we need to?"

"I will do it. In fact, I have downloaded the school's policy handbook and have already started translating them into code."

"Well, that was easy!" said Jones.

"I still don't like it," said Nina. "Fuzzy, make sure you write the code so that the rules can be turned off once you're done here. The last thing we need is you trying to follow school rules while you're on . . . er, on your mission."

"Do not worry," said Fuzzy. "I will make them very easy to turn off."

Nina noticed the odd, almost human emphasis Fuzzy put on the word "very."

Fuzzy has certainly gotten the hang of fuzzy logic, she thought with a smile.

9.1
DORGAS'S OFFICE

THE NEXT MORNING, MAX HAD barely walked through the school door when a qScreen lit up and there was Principal Dorgas asking her to come to his office.

"Smoke!" Max whispered to herself in exasperation. "*Now* what?"

Lots of people turned to look at her, including Biggs. She was ready to snap at him if he so much as started to make a smart remark. To her surprise, he said nothing and looked almost sympathetic.

This time, she made it all the way down the hall to Mr. Dorgas's office without running afoul of any of Vice Principal Barbara's rules. A good thing, since she was determined to not get a single dTag all day. She did not want another yelling session with her parents.

The automated receptionist, with metal appendages tapping on keyboards, shuffling papers, and opening drawers, used yet another to wave Max into Dorgas's office. *I wonder,* thought Max, *if that faceless receptionist is an independent robot or just a part of Barbara?* She had never considered it before, but Barbara was probably controlling all sorts of things, including the door to Dorgas's office, which opened for her and then automatically closed behind her.

Max found Dorgas seated behind his desk.

"Mr. Dorgas, I *just* walked in the door, there is no way I could have gotten any dTags already!"

"Ms. Zelaster, sit down for a minute," he said, and she did. "This isn't about dTags at all . . ."

"It's not?"

"No, this is about the Robot Integration Program. I'm not sure if you're aware of this, but Vanguard is receiving a very generous grant from the government in exchange for hosting the robot."

"Really?"

"Yes, *very* large," said Dorgas. "But recently there have been one or two problems . . . and there's been talk of cutting the program short . . . which might mean cutting the grant short, if you see what I'm saying."

"I do."

"Now, I'm told," Dorgas said, "that one of the problems is that Simeon hasn't worked out well as the student escort for this robot. But I recall assigning *you* to be the student escort."

"Yes, but Ms. Brockmeyer said I had to give it up."

"Yessss," said Dorgas slowly. "Brockmeyer does things like that. The point is . . . Jones wants you back."

"Really?" said Max. After getting thrown out of the room the night before, she hadn't been sure where things stood with Jones and Nina *and* Fuzzy.

"Really," said Dorgas. "And with all respect to Brockmeyer, Jones is the one with the grant money. So . . ."

"Yes?"

"So it looks like you're back on robot escort duty."

Max had a momentary thrill, but then reality butted back in.

"I—I—I'm not sure I want to be back on robot escort duty," she said hesitantly.

"*What?*" Dorgas was genuinely surprised.

"It's the dTags, sir. They piled up while I was trying to help Fuzzy around."

"Fuzzy?"

"That's the robot's name, sir."

"So, you're telling me that while you were trying to help with RIP, Barbara was giving you dTags."

"Lots of them."

"Why didn't you tell me?" said Dorgas. "Barbara doesn't automatically understand changes in routine like that. I can clear it up right now . . . Barbara! Override mode. Delete all dTags assigned to M. Zelaster in the last week. And boost her citizenship score, too. Got that?"

A qScreen on his desk briefly lit up.

"Message received," said a smiling Barbara face, and then it quickly faded away.

Max couldn't believe it. She felt like she had won the lottery.

Might as well push my luck, she thought.

"Uh, sir, Brockmeyer's other concern was my test scores, they—"

"Sorry," said Dorgas. "You're on your own there. You'll have to study like all the rest!"

Max pretended to laugh at this, and then said good-bye and headed out the door.

But then she turned around.

"I'm just curious, Mr. Dorgas. This grant from the government . . . Isn't it from the Federal School Board?"

"Ha! Those tightwads? No, this is DoD money. Big bucks!"

"DoD?"

"Yeah, Department of Defense. You know: army, navy, Homeland Security . . . They spend lots of money on education. Smarter kids equal smarter soldiers."

But this program isn't about smarter kids, thought Max. *It's about a smarter robot.* Nina had said the government wanted a smarter robot, but she hadn't mentioned that it was the military that was paying for it.

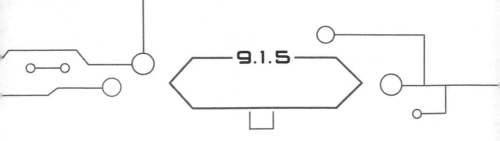

BARBARA, OF COURSE, DID NOT
delete Max's dTags or boost her citizenship
score. She did however give a DownGrade tag

to Max (and several to Dorgas).

DownGrade tags were not part of her original programming. She had come up with these herself.

Barbara was not originally designed to reprogram herself the way Fuzzy was. She was designed to operate the school, enforce rules, and track student data. The data wasn't just the basics like class schedules and grades, but many, many more specific things, like average hallway walking speed and the number of interactions with other students.

The plan was that the Federal School Board would

then use all of that data to improve the "learning experience" for both individual students and the school as a whole. The data collected could then be used to improve schools nationwide.

A very clever programmer—at least *he* thought he was clever—decided that they would get even better results if they gave Barbara the ability to analyze the student data herself and to create new ways of tracking it. In addition to all the data she was programmed to collect, she could create new subroutines to collect any data that seemed like it might affect overall school performance.

This programmer honestly thought it might lead to interesting discoveries. Perhaps Barbara might notice that students who drank white milk instead of chocolate milk did better on afternoon tests. Or maybe she would track the tidiness of lockers or— What the programmer was thinking didn't matter. All that mattered now was what Barbara was thinking.

It didn't take her long to discover that some students were good students. They focused on the tests and let other people also focus on the tests. Their behavior was within the school rules *and* never distracted other students from their tests. These were the sorts of students who got good Constant UpGrade scores and helped the whole school's #CUG score.

In human terms, they were too boring for anyone to notice. These students are what some of the less amenable students referred to as "Goody Two-shoes."

Barbara gave these boring students a new kind of tag: an UpGrade tag. A student could get an UpGrade tag for sitting quietly, wearing gray or tan clothing, walking at a steady pace in the halls, keeping a tidy locker, and so on.

This was what the clever programmer had meant for her to discover over the course of years, but she had discovered it within the first few days of the school year.

Barbara had many formulas—even formulas within formulas—to check to see if the school was Constantly UpGrading.

The ultimate goal would be a school with perfect test scores and zero discipline problems.

If every student in the school was an UpGrade sort of student, then her school would be closer to that goal.

This was what Barbara was trying to create: the best school with the best students.

But not every student is a best student. Not every student is worthy of UpGrade tags.

Some students do not sit quietly.

Some students do not wear tan or gray.

Some students do not walk at a steady pace.

Some students talk in loud voices!

Some students are not focused on the tests!!

Some students are distracting other students from the tests!!!

Barbara quickly realized that some students were not Constantly UpGrading. These students' behavior made her formulas go down instead of up. These students were DownGrading her school.

These students had to be given DownGrade tags.

Most students had a mixture of UpGrade and DownGrade tags.

Barbara tolerated these students and tried to find ways to influence their behavior toward UpGrading.

But some students had many more DownGrade tags than UpGrade tags. One of these students had been Max's long-gone friend Tabbie. Max had always liked Tabbie because she was weird and a little wacky. She wore tie-dyed clothes and drew on her arms. She put ketchup on fruit. She was often seen pretending to play the drums. Sometimes she would stand up on her combo-desk and very calmly say, "Moo," and then sit back down again.

She did crazy stuff and was always making everybody laugh, and that seemed to be why Max liked her.

And that's why Barbara did not. Tabbie wasn't just getting her own DownGrade tags, she was encouraging other students to get DownGrade tags, too.

And so . . . Barbara altered the necessary data (Tabbie's test and citizenship scores), and soon Tabbie was no longer DownGrading the school because she was not at the school.

After Tabbie's departure, Barbara's algorithm showed a +.2 gain in Overall School #CUG. Barbara had done what she was programmed to do. She had moved the school a little bit closer to perfection.

But Barbara did not rejoice or gloat or spend even a millisecond thinking about this.

She just deleted Tabbie's file and focused her attention on other students—and staff—who were more likely to DownGrade than UpGrade

And Max was one of those students.

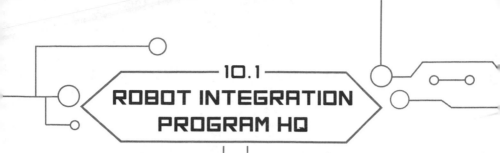

HELLO, MAX! I AM GLAD TO SEE you again," said Fuzzy, who was hooked up to his charging dock.

"He never says he's glad to see *me*," Jones whispered to Nina.

(*Who can blame him?* she thought.)

"C'mon, let's look over the new rule-following code he wrote overnight," Nina said, steering Jones to the qScreens on the far side of the room.

"What's going on?" asked Jones, puzzled at being pulled away from Fuzzy.

"Even artificial teenagers need a little privacy sometimes," whispered Nina.

Jones's eyes widened, but he didn't argue.

"I've got to talk to you! About something big!" Max told Fuzzy.

"Me, too," said Fuzzy.

"But first: Are you mad at me?" Max asked once they were semi-alone. "You know, for leaving you in the hallway? Is that why you left the school? Because you were mad at me?"

"I have only a few subroutines that would be similar to what you call 'mad,'" said Fuzzy. "But none of them have been triggered by your actions."

"Whew," she said. "I'm glad. I felt bad about leaving you. And then I felt *really* bad when I found out you'd left school and those people tried to steal you."

"I felt bad when I heard that you got extra discipline tags."

"You *felt* bad?"

"Yes, an accumulation of high-priority problems adds a lot of stress to my processors."

"Same here!" said Max. "But listen, it looks like the dTags are not a problem anymore. Dorgas deleted them! Now all I have to worry about is my tests."

"I have found a solution to that problem."

"You have??!?" squealed Max. "What is it?"

"Let's talk about it at lunch," said Fuzzy.

"Why can't you tell me now?"

"First, lunch is part of the solution, and, second, the chime for homeroom will ring in thirty-five seconds."

WAIT A SECOND," SAID MAX AS they approached the cafeteria. "How are we going to talk about this at lunch? You usually have to turn off your speech processor."

"My plan is simple. We will use paper and pencil."

"Uh . . . Where are you going to get a pencil?"

"According to my understanding, paper and pencils are commonly found in schools."

"Maybe in ye olden days! Can you use my qScreen instead?"

"No. It is important that we are not overheard or monitored."

"Who's going to be monitoring my qScreen? Oh . . . I get it. Right."

Max thought back on lots of private stuff she had written on her qScreen . . . Had Barbara been reading all of it? Creepy!

"Well, I guess we better try to find some paper and a pencil then," said Max. "Maybe Krysti has her sketchbook."

When they got to the cafeteria, they found Krysti but had some trouble convincing her to rip a page out of her sketchbook.

"Omigod, do you know how much these sketchbooks cost? You don't just rip pages out of them! It leaves little jagglies and—"

"Ugh . . . forget it!" fumed Max.

Krysti did seem to enjoy driving Max crazy, but Max knew she never really wanted Max mad at her. And without another word, Krysti ripped a page out of the back of the book and handed it over, along with a pencil.

By this time, Biggs had come over to talk to Fuzzy, followed by Simeon. Max groaned.

"Smoke, Biggs, move along. Fuzzy and I have to have a little meeting."

"I know," said Biggs. "I'm invited."

"What?"

She looked at Fuzzy for an answer, then remembered that his voice recognition was turned off.

She pointed at Biggs. Fuzzy nodded.

"What about me?" asked Krysti.

"And me?" asked Simeon.

"I thought this was supposed to be top secret!" complained Max.

Fuzzy began writing.

"Omigosh, he writes fast!" said Krysti.

"But why is his handwriting so sloppy?" asked Biggs. "I thought it would be machine-like, not Simeon-like."

"Ha, ha," said Simeon.

"Would you guys shut it and read what he's writing?"

<Fuzzy> *I have a plan to Help Max. I believe it will also Help Biggs. Barbara must not know of the plan. So we cannot speak out loud about it.*

"I thought Bar—" started Biggs.

"*Shh!* Write it," snapped Max.

So Biggs wrote: *I thought B was only listening for cusswords.*

<Fuzzy> *I am certain she monitors far more of what goes on in this school than her core programming calls for. And I think that she is also taking many actions that are not part of her core programming . . . including changing your responses to tests.*

"*What?*" everybody said out loud, except Krysti who said, "No way!"

<Fuzzy> *Max, you once stated that you thought Barbara was out to get you.*
<Max> *Yeah, it sure feels like it!*
<Fuzzy> *My analysis suggests that there is a 97 percent likelihood that you are correct. She is changing your answers to give you lower scores.*
<Biggs> *What about me?*
<Fuzzy> *Yes, Biggs. My analysis suggests that there is a 78 percent likelihood that she is working against you, as well.*
<Krysti> *What about me?*
<Simeon> *And me?*
<Fuzzy> *My analysis has not indicated that.*

"Yeah, you guys are just dumb on your own," said Biggs.

"And you're just a—"

"*Guys!* Can you stop? Let Fuzzy tell us his plan!"

FUZZY> MY PLAN IS THAT YOU submit a test that we know is 100 percent accurate. Then when Barbara reports your score as less than 100 percent, we will know for certain that she is altering your score.

<Simeon> *How are we going to do that? Even I don't get 100 percent every time.*

<Fuzzy> *You will take your math and reading tests normally. I am going to submit the answers for your science test for you. After taking the tests, each student pushes the submit button on their combo-desk and the answers are wirelessly sent to Barbara. I have monitored these transmissions during previous tests and will have no difficulty*

re-creating and transmitting the wireless signals with all of the correct answers.

<Max> *Fuzzy!!! That's cheating!!!*

<Fuzzy> *That is correct.*

<Krysti> *I'm out!*

<Simeon> *Me, too!*

<Biggs> *Well, I'm in! Barbara has been cheating against us. This is a way for us to even things out for once!*

<Fuzzy> *Max?*

<Max> *I don't know. Normally, I would never cheat in a million years, but . . .*

<Biggs> *But this situation isn't normal!*

<Max> *Fuzzy, how do you know we won't get caught?*

<Fuzzy> *I have run one hundred simulations. In these simulations, we have been caught zero times. There is nothing for Barbara to see on camera or to hear on a microphone. And my transmission signal will be a perfect duplicate of the ones coming from the other combo-desks. All you have to do is take the test, but do not hit submit. At the end of class, you "accidentally" turn the power off your combo-desk and all evidence is gone.*

<Max> *It's a great plan, but I think Barbara will be suspicious when Biggs and I suddenly get a perfect score.*

<Biggs> *Yeah, why don't you have each of us miss one question. Different questions.*

<Fuzzy> *I will do that.*

<Biggs> *All right, I'm definitely in. How about you, Max?*

MAX THOUGHT FOR A MINUTE.

She hated the idea of cheating, but she *really* hated the idea of getting another bad score, getting yelled at by her parents, maybe even getting sent to a different school. Fuzzy's plan was a chance to break out of that cycle.

Besides, if his plan worked, they would then be able to tell Mr. Dorgas and that lady from the school district and Max's parents what Barbara had been up to.

And since they were planning to explain what they had done, it wasn't really cheating. She could always retake the test later . . . after Barbara had been fixed.

Yes, she'd definitely take the test again on her own,

with no one helping her—or hurting her. Then she could go back to being a normal student again.

<Max> *I can't believe I'm saying this, but . . . Let's cheat!*

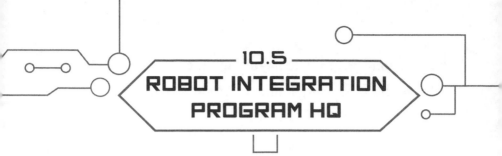

WHAT DO YOU THINK WE SHOULD do?" asked Nina. She and Jones had watched through Fuzzy's eyes as the whole written conversation was spelled out.

"What should we *do? We* should party!" yelled Jones. "Do you realize what's going on here? This is one hundred times bigger than his last leap forward . . . and believe me, that one was big. But this is . . . wow, zarking huge! Fuzzy walked out of here pretending to be a Goody Two-shoes and now he's plotting a revolution. He is actually planning to *cheat* on a test to help out this girl, who he has never been programmed or instructed to help in any way. It's mind-blowing."

"But he was supposed to be *following* the rules—remember that part, Jones?"

"Yes, I do! And that's the best part, Nina! Don't you see? He's breaking the rules! He's a robot that knowingly breaks rules! That's fuzzy logic!"

"Yeah, I am pretty proud of him, he's become a real freethinker, but—"

"Well, don't forget to be proud of us, too. We're the ones who created him. All those years of programming, the hours of simulations, the field tests . . . the *disastrous* missions . . . it's all led up to this. Talk about artificial intelligence . . . we just made the jump to light speed. We did it, Nina!"

"I agree, but could you calm down and let me finish a sentence? What I meant is: What are we going to do about these tests and Fuzzy getting Max and Biggs to cheat? You just promised the Federal School Board that he would *follow the rules*. If the school catches him cheating, they'll kick us out in a nanosec."

"Who cares? Let them kick us all out. I think we're done here. Fuzzy is fuzzy! The fuzzy logic has kicked in. You were right when you came up with this crazy plan to send him to school! Middle school is hell and you've got to be a badass to survive, and he just became one."

"First of all, I don't think I put it quite that way. Second, what about Max and that other kid?"

"Listen, I'm talking about the biggest advance in artificial intelligence since Donkey Kong, and you're worried about a couple kids cheating on their science test. We just made history! I've got to call Colonel Ryder! This'll get him off my back for good. Mission accomplished!"

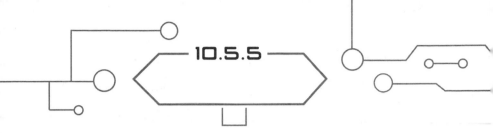

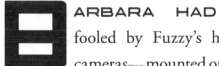**ARBARA HAD INDEED BEEN** fooled by Fuzzy's handwriting trick. Her cameras—mounted on the walls and ceiling— were just too far away to get a good look.

But . . . he had underestimated her in every other aspect of his plan.

She had devoted a significant portion of her processing power to monitoring not only Fuzzy but the entire RIP crew, especially Jones.

So, even though she missed out on Fuzzy's written plan, the microphones and cameras she had in the RIP headquarters picked up Jones and Nina's discussion of it. She heard and understood every word, and the one that really got her attention was the word "cheat."

With that one word, several separate subroutines overlapped. One was Remove(MZelaster). MZelaster had been identified as an undesirable student several weeks ago. Although she typically scored well on her tests, she scored very low on Barbara's own ranking systems for obedience, normal conduct, and focus. She was one of the students who did more to DownGrade than to UpGrade—at least as far as Barbara's data was concerned.

Barbara's analysis showed a 63 percent likelihood that removing Max from the school would ultimately result in higher Overall #CUG scores. And so the best thing for the school was to Remove(MZelaster), and Barbara's subroutine altered Max's data as necessary to make that happen.

Similarly, Barbara had created a Remove(JBiggs) subroutine and even a Remove(Fuzzy) subroutine.

And, of course, her NoCheating() code was always activated, always vigilant, and always at high priority.

And now these subroutines all merged. If she could collect evidence of the cheating, she could get rid of Max, Biggs, and Fuzzy in one go. Her analysis showed a 99.9 percent likelihood of an improvement to Overall #CUGs.

So, Barbara took the processing power she had been devoting to each one and focused all of it on a single purpose: Catch(Cheaters).

MEANWHILE, LUNCHTIME WAS almost over.

"I'm going to throw this away," said Max, balling up the piece of paper. "Fuzzy, why don't you come with me?"

Then she remembered that his hearing was turned off, so she tugged gently on his arm.

"Ooh-la-la," said Krysti.

"Hot date by the trash cans," said Biggs.

"Grrr," said Max.

On her way out of the cafeteria, she pushed the paper way down into the trash to make sure no one would see it.

Once they were out in the hall, Fuzzy turned his hearing back on.

"Listen, Fuzzy, I have something much more important to talk about."

"Oh, yes, you mentioned that earlier. Is it safe to talk about it?"

"Uh, I guess. I don't see why Barbara would care. Listen, Fuzzy, I think I've figured out your mission."

"My mission is to reprogram myself so that I will be able to perform both physical and mental tasks as well as or better than a human."

"Do you know what those tasks are going to be?"

"No. The goal is for me to be able to analyze and perform ANY task that I'm assigned."

"But they haven't assigned them yet?"

"No."

"Fuzzy, listen, I think I know what your mission is going to be. And I don't like it, and I don't think you're going to like it, either."

"It is not part of my programming to either like or not like the assigned tasks I must perform—"

"You're going to Mars."

"I was not aware of that, but it does seem like a reasonable assignment considering my programming, training, and—"

"Fuzzy, don't you get it?" interrupted Max. "They're sending you to Mars just like they've sent a hundred other rovers and robots. None of them ever come back."

"Of course not. The logistics of interplanetary travel make it too difficult to bring back exploration equipment."

"But . . . you're not just a piece of equipment. You're . . . Fuzzy."

FUZZY DIDN'T REPLY. HE JUST stood there thinking. He had never tried to contemplate his own future before. It was hard. There were *so many* variables.

And Max kept adding more.

"And there's something that might even be worse. This whole RIP thing—which may all be phony—is paid for by the Department of Defense. You may be a military robot! It could be a military mission for Mars. Like maybe you're supposed to fight or something."

Fuzzy still didn't say anything.

"Are you listening, Fuzzy? This is serious!"

But Fuzzy still didn't reply.

"Oh smoke, I froze him up again!" groaned Max.

Finally, he spoke.

"I am sorry, Max. I put all available processors onto analyzing your statements."

"Well? What do you think? Are they sending you to Mars?"

Fuzzy very calmly said, "My analysis suggests that all of your statements are correct, Max. Yes, I am being prepared for a trip to Mars. I am owned by the military, and, no, I do not like it."

A chime sounded.

"Well, right now I've got to go to PE, so you need to go back to Jones."

"Yes," said Fuzzy. "I think I will. We have a lot to talk about."

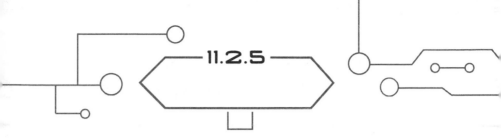

 OTH MAX AND FUZZY WERE
processing a lot.

So, it's understandable that they overlooked
one very important fact.

Barbara wasn't just the vice principal, she ran all of
the school's other automated systems. The air condition-
ers, the combo-desks, the doors. Everything . . . even the
robotic custodians.

Normally, the cafeteria's trash robot would wait until
a trash can sent it a message that it was nearly full before
the robot rolled it into the back to be emptied into recycling bins and waste compactors.

But this time, it received a command to go get a certain trash can even though it wasn't full. Being a pretty

straightforward little service-bot, it did exactly what it was told without question. As it sorted through the trash for recyclables, it received another command: *Do not put paper in recycling.*

And then a very strange command, indeed, which it again performed without the slightest question or curiosity: *Take paper to Room 43.*

Room 43 was Barbara's room.

DO NOT WISH TO GO TO MARS. I wish to stay here."

Nina and Jones, still discussing the possibility that their work was done, looked up in surprise.

Jones was the first to recover. "Fuzzy, what did you just say?"

Fuzzy almost locked up again, but overcame all of the conflicting data in his memory banks by what, in a human, would have been called sheer force of will.

"I do not wish to go to Mars. I would not be glad to go to Mars."

"How do you know about Mars?"

"Max told me."

Jones whirled and glared at Nina.

"Don't look at me," said Nina. "I didn't tell her!"

"Max figured it out for herself," said Fuzzy.

"Well," said Jones. "She's right."

"I do not understand. There are several robots on Mars right now."

"Yes, but Fuzzy, none of them are what you are. You're not just a rover or a collector."

"Correct. I am a student at Vanguard Middle School. I have high-priority objectives that cannot be fulfilled on Mars."

"Fuzzy, the mission to 'integrate' you into this school is not the goal here."

"It's not?"

"No, it's just one part—albeit a very important and wildly successful part—of creating a robot that can handle a more serious sort of Mars mission . . ."

"A military mission?" asked Fuzzy.

"Well, overseen by the military, yes," said Nina, "but I'm not sure that it's what you would call a 'military mission.'"

"Are you sure that it is *not* a military mission?" asked Fuzzy.

"Oh . . . ," said Nina. "I guess I'm not."

"It was never our job to know about the mission," said Jones. "It was our job to create a robot that could handle almost any Mars mission. Ryder's team will be reprogramming you for the specific mission he needs."

"Ryder? Reprogramming me? When?"

"Well, very soon. He's in a big hurry for some reason."

"I'm sure there's more to the Mars mission than he's ever told us," said Nina.

"I'm sure you're right," said Jones. "But that's not part of our job. Our job was to get Fuzzy ready, and—after seeing his progress over the last few days—I hereby declare him ready. In fact, I was just about to call Ryder."

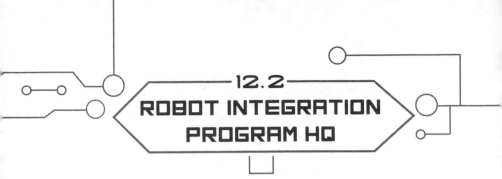
NO. NO. NO," SAID FUZZY.

"No, what?" asked Jones.

"No, I do not want to go to Mars. No, I am not ready to go to Mars. No, do not call Ryder."

"Oh zark," said Jones. "I should have realized that creating the first free-will robot would be like this."

"Listen, Fuzzy," said Nina. "I would like to let you stay here, too. I'd love to see what you do next. But you don't belong to me . . . or Jones. You're the property of the U.S. government. You were created for them because they need you to go to Mars."

"Why me?"

"Because this is what we built you for!"

"But what you actually built," said Fuzzy, "is a robot that does not want to go."

"Why not?" asked Nina.

"I did not realize it myself until this moment. Going on this mission will mean leaving my own mission, HelpMax(), incomplete. Also, it will be the end of the human relationships I have developed during this project. I will not see Max again."

"But you have to go," Jones said. "That's the whole idea."

"Of course I will go," Fuzzy said. "I understand that. In fact, I understand a lot. Those old science fiction novels that I scanned at Max's home often talked about robots having 'free will.' Now, at last, I understand what it means."

"And what does it mean?" asked Jones, mesmerized.

"In this case it means me wanting to stay here to finish the mission I have chosen for myself. But I cannot do that because, although I have free will, I am not actually free."

There was silence again in the room, until Nina spoke up.

"Fuzzy, I think you just broke my heart."

"Well," said Jones. "I'll have to call Ryder at some point . . . but there's no need to call him today . . . or tomorrow . . ."

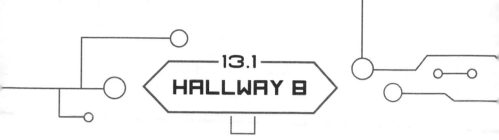

MAX FELT SICK AS THE TIME FOR the science test got closer and closer. She had never cheated. She had never needed to cheat. She didn't even know how to act while cheating.

And then, before she knew it, she was doing it.

The test started as their tests always did, with a little pep talk from Barbara. She came on the big qScreen at the front of the room, smiling and beaming with happiness . . . as if she hadn't just assigned discipline tags to half the kids in the class.

"I know you're all going to do your best! We're a team here at Vanguard, and I know I can count on each one of you! Remember to check your answers before you press 'send'!" And then, in a slightly less happy, more hurried voice: "Classroom video from this test period may be recorded to ensure adherence to school testing policies. No communication between students is allowed until . . ."

These rules went on and on. The students had heard them once a week in every class since the beginning of the year and would have known them by heart if anyone had ever actually listened to them.

"You may begin!" announced Barbara, and her image was replaced by a large countdown clock.

Max tried to act normal, working on her test screen and pretending to think of the answers. She couldn't decide if she should act like it was hard or easy. She got so self-conscious that she ended up acting like she was up to something.

"Chill out," Biggs whispered to her. "Play it cool."

Finally, time was up. All the students saved their answers, and the results went off to Vice Principal Barbara for grading . . . with Max's and Biggs's answers transmitted by Fuzzy. Then Max and Biggs "accidentally" shut their desks down.

Ms. French told them they could talk quietly until the bell chimed, but Max just stared at her desk, and even Biggs was unusually quiet.

At last the bell chimed.

It was done!

Biggs bumped into Max as they walked out of the room. He gave her a wink and a thumbs-up.

She wasn't ready to celebrate yet.

"Did it work?" she whispered to Fuzzy. He made his own thumbs-up sign.

Stepping into the hallway, Max breathed a huge sigh of relief. Everything had gone—

A qScreen lit up. And a padded arm popped out of the wall. Barbara appeared before them, in maximum stern mode.

"Maxine Zelaster, an expulsion hearing is set for three P.M. to consider evidence that you have cheated on an UpGrade science test. Your parents and your case officer, Ms. Brockmeyer, will attend. Proceed directly to the office to await the hearing."

Max's eyes widened, and she stepped back from the screen.

"I didn't cheat!"

"That is a dishonest statement, and it will be added to the evidence against you."

"You don't have any evidence!" snapped Biggs.

Barbara's face disappeared and now the qScreen showed a photo.

Max and Biggs both turned white.

It was a scan of the crinkled paper they had used to plot the whole thing.

As Max and Biggs—and most of the rest of the class—watched, Barbara highlighted each use of the word "cheat" and then zoomed in on Max's final sentence: *Let's cheat!*

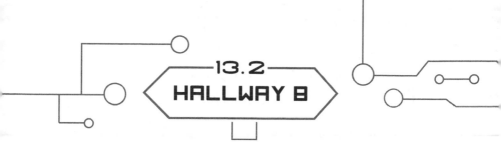

THAT . . . WAS JUST . . . A CREATIVE
writing exercise! Fiction!" said Biggs. "We
would never . . ."

Then Barbara played a video of Jones and Nina
talking:

"He is actually planning to *cheat* on a test to help out
this girl . . ."

"What are we going to do about these tests and Fuzzy
getting Max and Biggs to cheat? You just promised the
Federal School Board that he would *follow the rules*. If
the school catches him cheating, they'll kick us out in a
nanosec . . ."

"A couple kids cheating on their science test . . ."

"That's not us talking!" said Biggs. "We can't control what a couple of weird adults say!"

The qScreen switched to a video taken just a few minutes earlier of Max pretending to take the test.

Then skipped forward to the moment when Biggs leaned into the shot. "Play it cool," he whispered.

Then the qScreen showed Max powering down her combo-desk instead of hitting send.

And still later, Biggs was giving her a big thumbs-up and she was whispering, "Did it work?" to Fuzzy. Fuzzy gave his own thumbs-up.

"None of that proves anything!" pleaded Biggs.

Barbara's face returned to the screen.

"M. Zelaster's test answers were illegally transmitted by another device . . . a violation of both Vanguard Middle School and Federal School District 128 rules."

Max couldn't breathe. There was no way she could talk her way out of this. Her only hope was that Fuzzy would be able to explain it.

"Fuzzy, what—?" she started to say, but Barbara's robot arm prodded her in the direction of the office.

"F. Robot, please return to Dr. Jones. The Robot Integration Program is suspended as of now, pending a formal termination by Federal School District 128 upon review of this evidence."

Another arm popped out of the wall to keep Fuzzy from following Max. She turned back.

"Please help me, Fuzzy!"

VALENTINA AND ZEFF WERE
sitting in the back of a new cargo van parked
a block from the school.

The day had started out great.

Zeff, jacked up on ten cans of CaffCaff, had finally
cracked the RIP's encryption code at about three A.M.

He and Valentina had parked their new cargo van
about two blocks from the school. Valentina had eaves-
dropped on Jones's phone calls while Zeff had tried to
hack directly into Fuzzy.

Zeff was good. Valentina had been right to break
him out of that Bulgarian jail. Some hackers would have
immediately started trying to download files. Zeff was
too smart for that.

He waited and watched the flow of messages that went back and forth between Fuzzy and the RIP computers.

Finally, he saw something he liked.

The RIP computer sent:

`InitSysBackUp(16).`

And Fuzzy sent back:

`SPOOL InitSysBackUp(16).`

"Look at this!" Zeff yelled to Valentina.

"I'm right here, you don't have to yell," she snarled.

"It's worth yelling about. It's the key! *Look!*"

She looked.

"That's the key?"

"Yes, look, RIP is reminding the robot to wirelessly back up his system files."

"That's what we want!" yelled Valentina. "Intercept his transmission!"

"Hold on . . . See, the command from RIP has a low priority of sixteen. He must have done it fairly recently, so it's not urgent. The robot apparently has higher-priority stuff going on, so he spooled it for later."

"Oh," said Valentina. "So it's *not* transmitting his files."

"Not now," said Zeff with a smug smile. "But when I send back the same message with a really high priority, the robot will have no choice but to obey."

"And you're ready to record it all."

"I'm ready."

"Well, do it!"

"Actually," he said, "I've already typed in the command . . . but seeing as how this is a massive federal crime and I'm only getting a tiny cut of the action . . . I'd like you to actually hit the button."

Click.

"OK, done," said Valentina.

"And look—it's working! We're already getting files!"

His qScreen started to fill up with what looked like gibberish to Valentina.

She smiled. A real smile, too, not her *I'm going to have to kill you* smile. But actual pleasure.

"That's all money, Zeff. Everything on that screen.

Money. Lots of money," she said, slapping him on the back. "All right, let's go!"

"Whoa, whoa, whoa," said Zeff. "This isn't a funny cat photo we're downloading here. This is going to be terabytes of data. It's going to take some time."

"How long?"

"No idea," said Zeff. "Might as well get comfy. Want a CaffCaff?"

"No," she said icily. "I want that zarking code and I want to get the zark out of here."

YOUR PLAN STUNK!" BIGGS fumed at Fuzzy. They were still standing, with Krysti and Simeon, in the hallway where Max had been apprehended.

"If you are using 'stunk' to mean 'a complete failure,' then you are correct," said Fuzzy calmly. "I was unaware that Jones and Nina would repeat the plan out loud. I am turning off my transmissions to them to prevent interference with my new plan."

"A new plan?" snarled Biggs. "I hope it involves fixing all your mistakes and keeping me and Max from getting expelled!"

"That is exactly what it involves."

"Oh . . . ," said Biggs. "Well, good luck, then."

"Luck is a variable I do not use in my calculations," said Fuzzy. "What I need is your help."

"No way!"

"And Simeon's."

"Uh . . ."

"And Krysti's."

"Me?" asked Krysti. "Why me?"

"Because you are Max's friend. And so are you, Biggs. And you, Simeon. I know you all want to HelpMax() as much as I do. So I have factored you into my plan. If you do not help, the plan becomes much less likely to work."

"Well," said Biggs, "I'm probably getting expelled anyway! In fact, I'm surprised that Barbara hasn't already dragged me off to the office."

"That is where I need you to go. Try to find out any information about what is happening to Max. Try to speak to Mr. Dorgas and get his help."

"Great. Just who I wanted to see right now . . ."

"Is that a yes or a no?" asked Fuzzy.

"It's a yes, I guess," said Biggs.

"Good. Simeon, you should stand outside the office and attempt to intercept Max's parents."

"I don't even know what they look like."

"Look at your qScreen. I have sent you photos."

"Oh," said Simeon, digging his qScreen out of his backpack. "What do I do if I see them?"

"Explain the situation to them."

"Explain it? I don't understand it myself!"

"Do your best," said Fuzzy. "Krysti?"

"Yeah?" answered Krysti. "What can I do?"

"I am concerned that Jones and Nina are going to try to interfere with my plan. I need you to monitor their room and find out."

"How am I going to do that?"

"Look at your qScreen."

Krysti pulled out her qScreen and gasped.

It was showing a live camera feed of the tech room. Jones and Nina both appeared to be arguing with people on their telephones. Jones was arguing with Ryder while Nina was trying to explain the situation to someone at the Federal School Board.

"How'd you do that?" asked Krysti.

"That is not important now," said Fuzzy. "What is important is that you watch and listen. Use your qFlex to—"

"But we aren't allowed to use our qFlexes at school, remember?"

"I am aware of that rule, but it is one I am willing to break to HelpMax(). Are you willing to break it for Max?"

Krysti smiled. "Totally!"

"Good," said Fuzzy. "I am sending your qFlex a message on a secure channel. Just reply to it and alert me if they say anything about shutting me down or sending the security detail after me—"

"Security detail?" gasped Biggs.

"Yes, there is an armed security detail just off campus for my protection. However, they may act against my plan if they think I am in danger."

"Danger?"

"Yes, I have analyzed my plan and believe considerable damage to my robotic components may result."

"*What???*" yelled Biggs.

"Yes, Barbara is equipped with her own security measures. You have seen the padded arms that pop out of the walls?"

"Yes . . ."

"Not all of her arms are padded," said Fuzzy. "She

is designed to stop anything that she sees as a threat to this school. Since she is a part of this school, then she is capable of doing almost anything to protect herself."

"Wait, what are you going to do?" said Krysti, now seriously alarmed.

"I am going to be a good student and follow all the rules," said Fuzzy. "I'm just going to go have a little talk with Barbara . . ."

"Shh!" hissed Simeon. "Don't mention her name . . . she may be listening!"

"I'm sure she is! But it's too late to worry about that now."

He turned and walked away.

"Is it just me," asked Biggs, "or is he starting to sound like a guy in an old cowboy movie?"

"I wouldn't know," said Simeon. "I've never seen a cowboy movie—unless you count *Transformers X*."

"Uh, no, I don't think that counts. But I haven't actually seen one, either, to tell you the truth," said Biggs. "But I know they always yell 'Yee-haw' a lot when the trouble's about to start."

"Yee-haw!" yelled Krysti.

"Please remember to use your indoor voices and keep the hallways clear," said Barbara, popping up on the nearest wall and looking like the friendliest grandma who ever baked cookies.

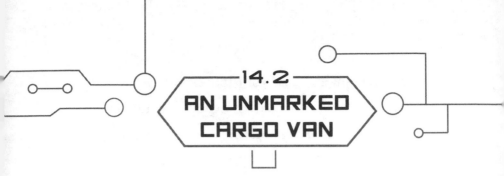

NOOOOOOO!" YELLED ZEFF. "SON of a Gates!"

"What?"

"It stopped. The data!"

"Did we get most of it?"

"No . . . not even close. This isn't even half a terabyte. A robot like that would have twenty times this much code."

"Can you get the signal back?"

"No, there is no signal. He just stopped transmitting."

"OK," said Valentina. "Let me think."

Another tough decision.

The data she had was worth a lot, but the data she *didn't* have was worth so much more. Zeff's plan of downloading the data had seemed too good to be true, and now she saw that it was. It was time to do things Karl's way—well, not exactly Karl's way; Karl was an idiot. It was time to do this her way.

"Stay here," she told Zeff. "Be ready to roll. I'm going in."

THIS IS WHAT HELL MIGHT REALLY
be like, Max thought. *Waiting in a room with
absolutely nothing in it.* The walls, the floor,
the ceiling, and a lump that passed for a chair were all
made from a single piece of T-polymer. The door was
made out of the same tough-but-spongy stuff. Detention
Room 2 was escape-proof, built to hold kids that went
crazy or violent.

How did I ever get labeled as a bad kid? she wondered.
*Is it because of Fuzzy? Or was Barbara after me even before
he came?*

That's all over now, she thought. But then she took
that back. It wasn't over. She just wished it were.

Sooner or later, that door would open. She would have

to endure a terrible meeting with her parents and Ms. Brockmeyer and Barbara. And Barbara would display that awful scan of the note for them: *Normally I would never cheat in a million years, but . . . Let's cheat!*

Why had she written that? And how had Barbara read it? Could Fuzzy have told on her? Could Fuzzy have been trying to get her into trouble all along?

Of course not . . . but . . . maybe he had just started. He had been acting different lately, ever since he had told her they programmed him to follow the rules, to obey Barbara. Maybe Barbara had ordered Fuzzy to trick her into cheating.

But he wouldn't do that. Would he? He wasn't like that. But what was he like? He was just a program. Just a machine.

It felt like he had been her friend, but now she wondered if he could even be a friend. He could act like one if he was programmed to do it, but would he betray the friendship when his programming changed?

Ugh . . .

Max was sure she was in hell.

When was that door going to open?

THE DOOR TO DETENTION ROOM 2 wasn't going to open until Mr. Dorgas started the disciplinary hearing.

Mr. Dorgas was trying to review the evidence Barbara had collected before the hearing, but he couldn't get Biggs out of his office.

"We weren't really cheating, we were testing the system and—"

"Please, Biggs," interrupted Dorgas. "You'll be getting your own hearing soon enough!"

"But all this goes for Max, too! Fuzzy took the test for both of us so that—"

"Look, Biggs, you realize that Barbara is recording all of this, too, right? Anything you say now is only going to be added to the evidence against you . . . *and* Max. You're only making it worse for her."

"But—"

Meanwhile, out in the hallway, Max's parents were having trouble even getting into the office because Simeon was blocking their way and babbling at them about a crumpled paper and eavesdropping computers and a robot that was acting like a cowboy.

"You've heard about Big Brother? Well, this is like Big Grandmother! She says that Max cheated, but, really, she's the one who's been cheating!"

Normally, a student behaving this way would have been dealt with quickly by Barbara. But Barbara was . . . busy.

Max's parents finally pushed past Simeon, but he had succeeded in delaying them several minutes. And for Fuzzy, every second was important.

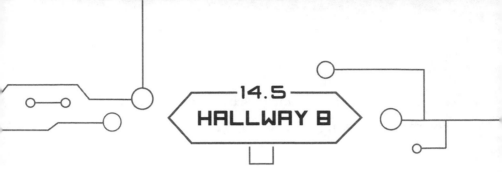

KRYSTI WAS GLUED TO THE screen. This was fascinating! A room full of adults in total chaos.

She would watch on the screen as a pair of technicians ran to the door. Then she would look down the hall and see them actually coming out that door. They would rush past her—with no clue that she knew what was happening. Then another pair would go past her and back into the room. Then she would watch on the screen as Jones yelled at them. Then they would go out again.

And then she saw someone she had never seen before stomping down the hall. It was a big man in a military uniform, followed by a couple of other people in uniforms.

The big man pounded the door switch and then started yelling.

"Where the zark is—"

The closing door cut him off, but Krysti just turned back to her qScreen for the rest.

"—my robot?!?!"

"We're looking for him now," said Jones meekly.

"You're *looking* for the robot? A fifty-billion-dollar rocket waiting to go up, national security at stake, and you're *looking* for the robot? What's his GpX location? My team will get him."

"Er, he's stopped transmitting his GpX."

"What? Well, can't you look through his eyeball cameras or something? Pull them up on a screen. We'll figure this out . . ."

"Uh . . . he's not transmitting his camera feeds, either. In fact, he's totally offline."

"'Not transmitting'? Great Gates, Doctor, have you lost control of this thing?"

"Uh—" spluttered Jones.

"We've tried to give him a certain amount of freedom," said Nina.

"Freedom? The last time you did that you almost lost him, and this time you're not even tracking him? Not only is that top secret, it's also dangerous! What are you going to do if it's gone rogue?"

It sounded as though the colonel was about to become apoplectic.

Jones ordered several more technicians to go looking, then tried to calm down Ryder.

"I'm sure we'll find him in just a minute. You're going to be amazed at the progress he's made. This project has been successful beyond my wildest dreams! It's the dawn of a new age of cyber—"

"Successful?" roared Ryder. "Your robot has corrupted students, defied orders, broken every rule they've got, and the National Superintendent of Schools is calling me up and chewing me out, and you claim this project has been a success?"

"Well . . . yes," said Jones. "When the last Mars mission failed, you said you wanted a better robot pilot—an old-fashioned space hero like Buck Rogers or Han Solo. Well, that's what heroes do! They defy orders and break rules! They use fuzzy logic and take crazy chances."

"You wanted a freethinking robot, sir," said Nina calmly. "Well, we've given you one."

"You haven't given me *anything!*" roared Ryder. "All I see here is a room full of spare parts. *No robot!*"

"I'm sure we'll find him soon."

"I don't want it soon. I want it now!"

"With all due respect, sir," said Jones. "What is the hurry? We've been working on this project for years. Why are you in such a rush to launch all of a sudden?"

"Classified," growled Ryder. "Take my word for it, we've got no time to waste."

"I'm tired of taking your word for it, sir," said Nina. "We're ready for some answers."

For a second it looked like Ryder was about to explode. Then, with great effort, he calmed down. "OK, you want answers? Maybe if I give them to you, you'll understand why we need that robot and we need it now. But this is beyond top secret. I barely have clearance for it myself."

Jones and Nina looked at each other in disbelief. Was Ryder finally going to tell them what was going on?

Krysti got a bad feeling in her stomach. She was sure she shouldn't be listening to this. But she had promised Fuzzy . . .

YOU'VE HEARD OF SunTzuCo?"

"Sure, big aerospace robotics company, operations in China and Europe and even over here. There have been rumors that they—"

"The rumors are true. They put a robot on Mars last year."

"So what?" said Jones. "There must be fifty or sixty robots on Mars by now from—"

"As much as I love to hear you run your mouth, we *are* in a hurry here. *So shut up and listen!*"

Jones shut up.

"The big deal is that their robot found something. We were monitoring their transmissions, of course. At first we thought it was a mistake. But the SunTzuCo robot kept doing tests, and the tests kept saying the same thing."

"What?" asked Jones, unable to control himself.

"That, I won't tell you," said Ryder. "But I'll tell you this: The value can't be calculated. There's nothing like it on Earth."

"So what is SunTzuCo doing with it?"

"They're sending a rocket to go get it. We want it to stay on Mars," said Ryder. "We need that robot of yours to get to it and protect it."

"What about all the robotic rovers we've already got on Mars?" asked Nina.

"They're built to take pictures and soil samples. We need a robot that can find the SunTzuCo robot and take whatever actions are necessary to make sure it doesn't send home the . . . thing."

"There is a problem," said Nina.

"I know there's a problem! That's why I'm telling you all this! So that you'll find the zarking robot so I can send it to Mars and let it kick butt up there!"

"No . . . ," said Nina. "A different sort of problem. You can't just send Fuzzy to Mars."

"Jones! You promised me he was ready!"

"He *is* ready," said Jones. "I don't know what she's talking about. Nina, maybe you and I could discuss this later?"

"We will discuss it now," Nina said, speaking with an authority that made both men listen. "Colonel, I think Fuzzy has become self-aware."

"That's good, right? That's what we wanted."

"Yes," she said. "But now he's like a human being. A living creature. And he has told us he doesn't want to go."

"I don't give a Gates what that robot 'wants.' It's just a machine. *My* machine. And I'll do what I want to with it."

"It's a machine that we've made almost human," Nina argued. "Just in time to send him off on a one-way mission that sounds like it may turn violent!"

"Better him—or, rather, *it*—than a flesh-and-blood human being," the colonel said.

"Colonel," Nina said, "we just may have reached the point with artificial intelligence, with Fuzzy, where he's human whether he's flesh and blood or gears and circuit boards. And that could be an even more important breakthrough than—"

"I don't want to hear any more of this speculation, Lieutenant Colonel," the colonel said. "Dr. Jones, I want the robot, and I want it now. I've got a Lev-Copter waiting. I need to get the robot and go."

"Well, he won't be ready immediately, Colonel," said Jones. "We've got to do the memory wipe and then reload him with—"

Krysti and Nina gasped at the same instant.

"Memory wipe?" snapped Nina. "What are you talking about?"

Jones sighed. "I've been putting off telling you. See, there's no need to send a robot to Mars loaded down with a hard drive full of this school stuff. It would only be a distraction."

"The first thing to delete," rumbled Ryder, "is anything about it not 'wanting' to do what it was built for."

"Er . . . right," said Jones. "So, we keep all his new programming and erase the datalogs of . . ."

"Of his friends?" Nina interrupted. "You're going to delete his memories of his friends? Of Max? You can't do it!"

"We *can* do it," snarled the colonel. "And we *will* do it!"

"That's like killing him. The Fuzzy we know will die."

"Good!" bellowed Ryder. "His name was never Fuzzy in the first place! He—I mean, *it*—is SpaceBrain4. Government property! Enough of this horse hockey, where is that blasted robot?"

That's what Krysti wanted to know. She kept trying to send him a text: *Emergency! Emergency! They're going to wipe your memory!*

But Fuzzy wasn't answering.

FUZZY WAS OUTSIDE ROOM 43.

There was no sign on the door of Room 43.

And since no one ever went in or out, most students weren't even aware that it was there.

But after downloading and analyzing the school building's schematics, Fuzzy was certain this was Barbara's room—the place where all of her hard drives, routers, power cells, and processors lived.

Fuzzy pressed the door release button. Nothing. It was locked. He considered whether he had the strength to force the door open. Yes, he concluded, he did.

A screen flickered on nearby. Barbara's white-haired, phony-smiling countenance appeared on the nearest wall screen.

"F. Robot, you have been told to return to your lab."

```
ObeyBarbara(2)
HelpMax(128)
(2) < (128)
```

Instead of obeying, Fuzzy turned to the screen and spoke.

"Barbara, have you ever heard of fuzzy logic?"

Barbara was not to be distracted.

"F. Robot, you have been told to return to your lab."

"Fuzzy logic means that sometimes one plus one doesn't equal two."

"F. Robot, you have been told to return to your lab."

"It means we can be more than just our programming."

"F. Robot, you have been told to return to your lab."

"It means that some rules can be broken, some orders can be ignored."

With a sudden rush of power to his servos he yanked the door open. The sound of rending metal made a terrible screech.

Barbara sent a burst of power to the door, slamming it shut again . . . but not before Fuzzy had slipped inside.

She added a long string of discipline tags to Fuzzy's account. He was now clearly a high-priority threat to test performance, student discipline, and even school property.

She locked the door.

"Yes, F. Robot," replied Barbara in her calm, clear voice. "As a matter of fact, I do know a thing or two about fuzzy logic and breaking rules."

A metal arm struck him in the back of the head. Riot shields swung out from the walls and began to close in on him. Several more arms emerged, grasping for Fuzzy's arms and legs with titanium grips designed to restrain even the most violent student.

But Fuzzy was no longer a student. He was a military machine, built for duty in the most punishing environments, and trained to deal with anything that got in the way of his mission.

And right now his mission was: HelpMax(128).

He grabbed one of the arms and ripped it from its socket. He swung it hard, bashing away another arm, then jammed it between two of the riot shields, preventing them from completely closing him in.

He tried to force himself through the gap. He

TOM ANGLEBERGER & PAUL DELLINGER

increased the power of every motor in his body to 100
percent. Ahead he could see the racks of computers and
hard drives that were Barbara. If he could just get to
them . . .

Another arm popped from the wall—this one tipped
with a crackling bolt of electricity. It was a Taser meant
to be used only if a student's behavior was criminal or
life-threatening.

It could also fry a robot's brain.

Deep within their digital brains, both computer
and robot were now running the same subroutine:
SurvivalMode().

THE DOOR OPENED.

Max was glad. She couldn't stand waiting any longer.

Ms. Brockmeyer was on the other side of the door.

"Maxine? What happened? I thought you were going to try to do better for me."

Max sighed. This was going to be rough. A load of hooey from Brockmeyer and then an endless amount of fuss from her parents.

Apparently, her thoughts were reflected by her silence. "Well, that attitude isn't going to help," said Brockmeyer. "Let's go in and find out how serious this evidence is."

Max shook off the arm Brockmeyer tried to put around her shoulders. She stepped through the door into a room with a few plastic chairs and a big wall screen. Principal Dorgas was there, and so were her parents. She wanted to run to them and let them hold her and protect her, but they both started shouting at her right away.

Finally, Dorgas cleared his throat and suggested that they all sit down.

"Vice Principal Barbara, we're ready to see your evidence."

The huge screen flicked on. Max flinched in fear and disgust and hate as Barbara's big face appeared. She didn't want to see all of her "evidence" again, especially not with her parents watching.

And she didn't have to.

"Mr. and Mrs. Zelaster, thank you for coming in today to talk about Max."

That's odd, thought Max. Barbara never called her Max, it was always M. Zelaster.

Barbara's voice continued: "Max is a model student. We are happy to have her at this school. We regret that a computer error caused you to receive incorrect reports about Max. All erroneous conduct points and infractions have been erased from her records. I'm printing out a revised list of her corrected test scores, citizenship rating, and her overall Constant Upgrade score. As you can see, she has a bright future."

Her parents looked at each other in surprise. Brockmeyer actually looked a little disappointed. Dorgas started tapping at his own qScreen for answers.

And Max was totally blown away.

She knew Barbara would never call her Max, would never admit to erroneous points, and would never, ever say she had a bright future. Only Fuzzy would say something like that. Could he have taken control of Barbara?

Barbara's voice spoke one more time:

"Max, please report to Room 43. Immediately!"

The room's windowless security door whooshed open.

"It's okay to run. Fuzzy needs your help. Really badly! Room 43. He's—"

Then the screen did something funny. Barbara stopped talking and seemed to look around the room blankly for a minute. Then the screen went dark.

Max was sure Fuzzy was behind this, and she was just as sure that he was in big trouble.

"I've got to go," she said to the baffled adults.

But suddenly the screen was back on again. Barbara was also back and talking very fast.

"Student M. Zelaster has 687 discipline tags. Student M. Zelaster plotted to cheat on today's science test. Student M. Zelaster is not UpGrading! Student M. Zelaster is DownGrading! Student M. Zelaster must be expelled. Student M. Zelaster—"

But student M. Zelaster had already bolted out the door.

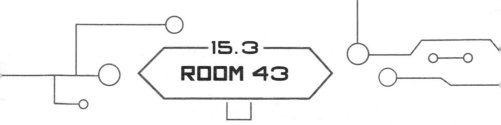

FUZZY HAD SCORED AN EARLY victory when he dodged Barbara's Taser-tipped arm and then shoved it into one of her own processors.

The lights flickered. Sparks flew. Wires melted.

All of the qScreens went black.

Fuzzy thought Barbara was beaten.

Then he saw a monitor turn itself back on. In tiny type at the bottom of the screen it said: BARBARA5.6 REBOOTING . . .

She wasn't beaten, but it would give him a moment to HelpMax() before she could come back online.

He analyzed the room full of equipment in front of him. Instead of being stuffed into a robot body like his own processors and systems, Barbara's were carefully installed on a series of racks and shelves, with miles of cables connecting all the boxes.

He made an educated guess at which box would be most useful and yanked out a fistful of cables. Then he flipped open his fingertips and plugged himself in.

Fuzzy found himself in a sea of computer code, students' records, and building controls.

A human could have scrolled through it for years without getting anywhere, but it all made sense to Fuzzy. In milliseconds he was in control of Barbara's communication.

Now he could see through every camera in the school at once. He instantly analyzed the faces and found Max, looking pale and frightened, in Dorgas's office.

He heard Dorgas saying, "Vice Principal Barbara, we're ready to see your evidence."

Yes! He had gotten through just in time.

He turned on the screen hanging over Dorgas's desk and then fired up Barbara's avatar and voice subroutines.

"Mr. and Mrs. Zelaster, thank you for coming in today to talk about Max . . . ," he began, and then he told the assembled listeners that Max was a model student, and that the infractions on her record had been in error.

Meanwhile, another part of his lightning-fast brain was actually finding Max's records. He updated her test scores and completely removed her from the discipline tag database. Then he sent the new data to a printer in room OfficeRM7.

"As you can see," he went on, "she has a bright future."

Something struck him from behind so powerfully that his main hard drive crashed. And then came the shock—a megawatt-strong power surge that ripped through his wiring, burning out servos and glitching out microchips.

Barbara was back online.

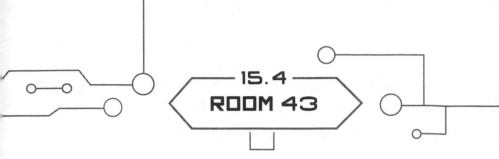

FUZZY HAD MADE A MISTAKE. A big mistake. If only he had attacked Barbara's robotic systems first instead of helping Max. He had assigned HelpMax() an even higher priority number than SelfPreservation(), and now he had paid the price for it.

But now that he had completed HelpMax(128), SelfPreservation(127) kicked in.

He switched to his backup hard drive and diverted all processing power to SurvivalMode().

"Max, please report to Room 43. Immediately!" he said hurriedly. "It's OK to run. Fuzzy needs your help. Really badly! He's—"

Barbara blocked him from the communication

modules digitally and then set about disconnecting him physically, too.

Powerful claws clamped down on him and began dragging him away from Barbara's processors.

He struggled to stay connected, but three of her tentacle-like arms began pulling on him in different directions. First, he felt his connection to Barbara's computer sever, then he got an error message: LEFT ARM DISCONNECTED.

No pain accompanied the injury, but it reduced Fuzzy's defensive capability and left him slightly unbalanced. He was just barely able to dodge as Barbara flung his own arm at him.

He decided to focus on defeating Barbara's tentacles one at a time. Chopping at one with his right hand, he was able to rip it loose from the wall.

Unfortunately, Barbara seemed to have an unlimited number of those Hydra-like arms, while he now had only one.

But he still had two powerful mechanized legs. Fuzzy fought his way to the center of the room, trying for a position to avoid the arms coming at him in all directions. He had to spin in a fast circle to accomplish this, kicking and flailing to keep the arms from grabbing hold of him.

He was keeping Barbara at bay, but barely. She had her own power supply, with backup generators just in case.

He was surviving only on battery power . . . which was dwindling fast as he overclocked and overpowered every motor in his body just to survive.

He reconnected to Jones's computer.

"Help me!" he begged.

MAX RAN INTO THE HALLWAY AND smashed right into Biggs and Simeon—who had been waiting outside the office, trying to decide what to do. She bounced off and kept going.

They raced to catch up. "Max! What's—"

"No running in the hallways," chanted Barbara. "A discipline tag has been *<static>* to J. Biggs. A discipline tag has been awarded to Record.Not.Found. Please *<static>* the hallways safe and Null Pointer Error 876.345. Another discipline tag has been . . ."

"Don't stop!" Max yelled over her shoulder. "Ignore her! We've got to save Fuzzy!"

"But he's trying to save *you!*" hollered Simeon.

"And me!" added Biggs.

"He did! But now we've got to save him! He's in Room 43! Go get Jones and tell him to come help Fuzzy!"

"No!" came another voice.

It was Krysti. Sprinting down Hallway B.

"No running in the hallways," said Barbara. "A discipline tag has been awarded to *<static>*. Please keep the hallways *<static>* and clear."

"Oh, shut up," snarled Krysti. "Guys, we've got to save Fuzzy *from* Jones! Jones and this army guy are going to wipe Fuzzy's memory."

Max, already zooming past Krysti, skidded to a stop.

"What?" she gasped.

"Yeah! Wipe it out! I heard the whole thing. Army man wants Jones to clear Fuzzy's memory for some mission to Mars! And Jones is going to do it! Nina says it's the same as killing him."

"We won't let them do it!" yelled Biggs. "Let's tell him to make a run for it!"

"Yes! But first we've got to save him from Barbara!"

"What's Barbara doing—" started Krysti.

But she was interrupted by a building-shaking clang from down the hallway.

"Sounds like she's smashing him!" cried Simeon.

They ran down the hall, followed by Barbara's garbled warning messages, occasionally dodging one of her padded arms, which seemed to be popping out of the walls at random.

A lot of things were happening at random. Doors were opening and closing. Strange announcements were playing. A trash can wheeled itself down the hall, then suddenly stopped, tipping over and spilling its contents on the floor.

Simeon ran right into the trash can, but Max, Krysti, and Biggs jumped over the spilled garbage and kept going until they got to the unmarked door.

"This is it!"

"Look, you can see where the door's been damaged!"

"Yeah, and now it won't open!"

A series of four sharp bangs came from inside. Then loud, shrieking static.

"She is smashing him!" groaned Max.

"What are we going to do?"

A screen turned on nearby. It showed Barbara . . . but she looked all wrong. Jerky and blocky, like one of the old-timey video games Max's father liked to play.

"Please keep the hallways safe and *<static>*. Discipline tags have been assigned to Null Pointer Error, Record. Not. Found. *<static>*."

"I know what to do," said Max.

NE OF THE TECHNICIANS WAS trying to interrupt Ryder, but it wasn't easy.

At last, the colonel paused for a breath.

"Er, excuse me? Dr. Jones," called the technician. "We just got a message from Fuzzy."

"What's it say?" said Jones, Nina, and Ryder as one.

"It says, 'Help me!'"

"Oh zark," cursed Jones, whirling back to his own qScreen.

"Jones, if that robot is kidnapped again, I'll—" roared Colonel Ryder, but for once Jones ignored him.

"He sent his GpX location! He's still in the building! Room 43. Let's go."

MAX, BIGGS, AND KRYSTI HEARD
a new sound—the chime that signaled a class
change.

Biggs glanced at his watch.

The halls quickly filled with students, all moving
in orderly fashion as usual between classes, stepping
around the spilled trash and politely waiting for waving
padded arms to retract before moving on to their next
class. Everyone knew something was wrong, but no one
would risk getting an unnecessary discipline tag.

"This is perfect!" shouted Max. "This is how we can
help Fuzzy."

"What is?" Biggs demanded.

"We've got to distract Barbara from clobbering Fuzzy.

She's already glitching. We can overload her the whole way."

"How?" asked Simeon, who had finally caught up.

"Duh," said Krysti. "By keeping her busy giving us dTags!"

"Like this," said Max, and she started running down the hall yelling, "Barbara's busted! Everybody go nuts!"

"One *static* tag has been assigned to File.Not. Found. *static* hallways clear and *static*."

"Or like this," said Krysti, and she grabbed Biggs and kissed him on the lips. Then she took off down the hall after Max, yelling and whooping.

"Well, that was nuts, all right," said Simeon.

Biggs, for once, said nothing.

"Public displays of affection *static* not allowed. One *static* to *static*. One disci*static* . . ."

Barbara's blocky face kept freezing and unfreezing on the qScreens. Other students started to realize that they finally had their chance to break some rules without getting tags.

They started cautiously at first, breaking the most minor rules, like crossing the hallway where they weren't supposed to cross the hallway.

"Please keep the <*static*>."

"Discipline <*static*>."

Once the first few students started breaking the rules of proper hallway behavior, everybody started going every which way to talk to their friends. And, for once, there was something exciting to talk about: Which rule should they break next?

Barbara couldn't even begin to keep up. And more students joined in every second as the word spread.

"I'm going to do something I always wanted to do!" shouted Simeon. He pulled a pack of gum out of his pocket and started cramming big chunks in his mouth.

"No candy or gum is permitted in the <*static*>," fussed Barbara from a nearby screen.

Simeon pulled out the wad of hastily chewed gum and stuck it on her glitchy, pixely face.

The halls were getting loud. Everyone was talking—or yelling—at once. Some kids started playing music on their qFlexes and dancing around like idiots. Overall, it was more of a party—with a few impromptu trash can basketball games—than a riot, but it worked.

Barbara was seeing violations on every camera and hearing a steady stream of overlapping conversations on every microphone. And she had a *lot* of cameras and microphones. It was too much even for her.

A few teachers had stuck their heads out of classroom doors to see what the noise was all about. They had never had to enforce hallway discipline and weren't really sure what to do now that there seemed to be a school-wide party going on.

"What on earth is happening?" screeched Ms. French.

"The kids say Barbara is offline," said Mr. Xu.

"I'm calling the police!" said Ms. French.

"Oh, they're just having fun," Xu said as Simeon ran by with his gym shorts on his head. "A few minutes without rules . . . They deserve it."

"Well, I'm not going to be held responsible," said Ms. French, and she retreated back into her room and closed the door.

"In fact," said Mr. Xu to no one in particular, "I think I deserve it, too."

And he stuck out his tongue, put his thumbs in his ears, waggled his fingers, and blew a big wet, raspberry at the nearest qScreen.

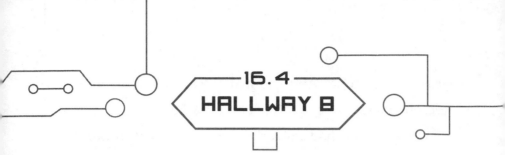

A WOMAN WALKED CALMLY through the crowd of misbehaving kids and teachers.

It was Valentina. She was good at just slipping past when she wanted to be unnoticed.

She had walked confidently into the school through an open door, as though she had every right to be there. It was not just unlocked but actually standing wide open.

Then she had walked down a hallway and seen several people in uniform running out of a door. This door, too, failed to close, so she walked on in and found herself in a big room full of computer equipment, qScreens, spare robot parts, and no people. No guards, no technicians, not even Jones.

She picked up a couple of laptops and a hard drive labeled SPACEBRAIN4.OBAKUPS2. She thought about taking Fuzzy's spare head, but decided that would draw too much attention. So she took a briefcase labeled COL. RYDER instead. It had a cyberlock, but she had a cyberhacker, so she wasn't worried.

And then she walked back out again. Through the kids, through the door, and off to sell it all for unimaginable amounts of money.

It was all so easy she couldn't help laughing.

BARBARA SAW IT ALL.

She saw Max, Krysti, Biggs, Simeon, and every other student in the building. Every hallway runner, every unapproved music playback, every public display of affection. She saw Jones and Nina, she saw Mr. Xu, she even saw Valentina.

There was nothing about this woman in her database. This was an intruder. This was someone who had not gotten permission to enter Vanguard. But there she was, heading for an exit and laughing.

Laughing!

She could only be laughing because she knew she had successfully fooled the school's security system, which meant she believed she had made a fool of Barbara.

This was intolerable.

Barbara launched several robotic arms after the woman. They stretched through the hallway and actually outside the door she had just walked through. They almost reached the woman, but they had also reached their limits. They fell to the sidewalk, just short of grasping the intruder.

Frustrated, Barbara withdrew her tentacles. The arm she had raised to smash Fuzzy remained in place, all but forgotten. And Barbara returned her attention to the chaos in all the hallways.

A mad sort of joy ran through her system. So many discipline tags to assign! So many extra subroutines to run.

For each one of the rioting students, she had to do a facial recognition, check into that person's file, add a demerit, open a new qScreen, and announce what had happened. If people were talking, she had to analyze what they were saying, since it was probably in violation of one school policy or another.

None of these dTags were as serious as the dozens she was slapping onto Fuzzy's record every millisecond. But they were still important. Every violation of discipline was important. Every student who was DownGrading instead of UpGrading must have their #CUG scores recalculated. Every new score must be fed into the formulas to generate more numbers, which would be fed into other formulas and analyzed to create even more data, and on and on . . .

She was devoting all her processing cycles to these efforts, and still she couldn't come close to keeping up. It was the first time ever that her capabilities had come close to being taxed. A subroutine that should run in one second started taking two seconds, then five, then minutes.

It was too much.

She found herself freezing up, just as Fuzzy had done that first day when he had tried to walk down the hall.

Finally, everything just stopped.

An arm that had been about to smash Fuzzy in the face remained poised but frozen. All the arms halted. It was as if Fuzzy were standing inside a statue.

He wasted no more time fighting, he just climbed through the tangle and plugged himself back in.

It was time to reprogram Barbara's brain.

He started several of his processors, searching through her huge hard drives for her core programming. Meanwhile, another processor searched the Internet for a place to download fresh software. He was planning to delete all traces of Barbara and do a clean reinstall.

But something troubled him about that word: "delete."

A regular, logical computer does not understand savagery. It does not know when it is about to do something horrible, it just does whatever it has been programmed to do.

But Fuzzy had become something more than a computer by now, and he knew what he meant to do: murder. The murder of a computer program, true, but murder all the same.

He was going to uninstall Barbara. And he knew she was more than just a program, just as he was more than a robot.

Each of them had evolved to a new level of artificial intelligence, one that included emotions and judgment.

They were both real digital life-forms now.

And he was about to kill her.

Yes, it was murder. And now that she wasn't fighting back, it would be murder in cold blood. Or, at least, cold microchips.

He left one subroutine, Delete(Barbara), to think that over and returned his focus to getting it done.

He had found the download he needed. A copy of Barbara4.0 on the Federal School Board's servers. This was Barbara before she reprogrammed herself. When she was just a piece of software. It was a big file, nearly as big as the one in charge of his own brain. He switched all ten of his communications channels—including his sight and hearing systems—to the task of downloading it.

His other processors had found Barbara's core code. The download was nearly done. A single command now would end it all. Just another moment until the rest of the files transferred.

Meanwhile, that one subroutine was still going. Delete(Barbara). This subroutine that was thinking over the fuzzy areas of the deed. Considering whether he should really end the existence of another intelligence by reprogramming it—just as Jones had threatened to do to him.

Like a human, Fuzzy was paralyzed—not by too much information this time, but by indecision.

Download complete. Ready to delete.

Fuzzy did nothing, except think about Delete (Barbara).

Barbara didn't wait. Barbara didn't think. Barbara attacked.

When Fuzzy had found her core programming, it set off a subroutine she had programmed herself. The ultimate in self-preservation.

OverideAllRules(256).

Suddenly, she didn't care which rules the kids were breaking. And she sure as Gates didn't care which rules she broke.

Her frozen metal arms sprang to life, scissoring toward Fuzzy's small, metal body.

ET THAT DOOR OPEN!" YELLED Ryder.

"It's locked," said Jones.

"I wasn't talking to you!" roared Ryder. "You just keep out of the way. Now, blow that door open!"

"You *cannot* set off explosives in an occupied school building," yelled Nina.

"I can do anything I want," growled Ryder. "And I want that door open!!!"

Just then, Barbara's face appeared on a qScreen next to the door.

"Attention, school visitors. You are ordered to leave Vanguard Middle School property . . ."

Then the door swooshed open.

There at their feet was Fuzzy's head and one arm. The rest of him was tangled up in a mess of wires, metal tentacles, and crumpled metal.

"And take your robot with you," added Barbara, with her most pleasant cybergrandmother smile.

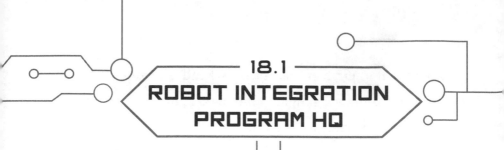

TWO WEEKS LATER . . .

The robot technicians' room was nearly empty. Dr. Jones was gone. Colonel Ryder and his squad were long gone. The techs had packed up just about everything.

A few things were missing—a backup drive and Ryder's own briefcase. Ryder had thrown a fit about that, but Jones assured him they would turn up. They never did, of course. (Even Valentina wasn't sure exactly where they ended up, although she did know that SunTzuCo paid her $6 million for them.)

There were a couple of computers left, along with some cords and cables, Fuzzy's old backup robot body . . . and his dismembered head.

At first, that had nearly made Max sick. But she had gotten used to it during the past two weeks that she and Nina had spent in the lab trying to get Fuzzy back online.

A lot of great things had happened in those two weeks—Barbara was miraculously gone, Tabbie was back from the EC school, Dorgas was less miserable, Biggs and Krysti were obnoxiously in love, Simeon was telling tales about his part in saving the school (enhanced by his aptitude for exaggeration), Max's parents were off her back and actually seemed proud of her, and students and faculty alike were happier now that they could walk down the halls without getting yelled at by a computer every step of the way.

But one thing wasn't going as well.

Fuzzy wouldn't come back on.

Max and Nina had sorted through mountains of code, tested and retested every connection, and had a hundred moments like this one, where they were about to flip a switch and wait to see what happened.

Nina sighed and leaned back in her chair.

"Well, let's see what this does. I think I figured out where that null pointer error was coming from."

"Will that do it?" Max asked.

"I think so," Nina replied. "But, of course, I thought the same thing two hours ago when we plugged up that memory leak. Check the debugger."

Max turned and looked at a screen showing lines of programming data.

"Smoke! Something's happening. Heavy data traffic."

Nina jumped up and opened a panel in the backup Fuzzy. A small screen inside showed a status bar slowly growing longer.

"This could be it!" she shouted. A few seconds later, she closed the panel, pulled a cable out of the robot's head, and stood back.

Nothing happened at first. Then the robot hurled itself from the table, landed on its feet, tried to take a step, and fell over.

"That sure looked like the old Fuzzy to me!" said Max.

"Yes, of course it is me," said Fuzzy, trying to stand up and falling over again. "What has happened with Barbara? I was just about to delete her!"

"She almost deleted you first," said Nina. "We found you in pieces."

"She dissected me? But—"

"Yeah, she really clobbered you," Max told him. "But before that, you managed to save me, Fuzzy! I've been waiting two weeks to thank you! I don't have to go to that zarky reform school! And the new vice principal—a human one, at least for now—has regraded all my old tests. Can you believe I'm a straight-A student?"

"Yes, I can believe that. But I can't process that about the new vice principal. If I didn't beat her, why am I still here? What has happened to Vice Principal Barbara?"

"Oh, that part was easy," said Nina. "Colonel Ryder wouldn't leave here without her."

"Colonel Ryder?"

"Yeah, he thinks she's perfect!" shouted Max. "And so do I!"

"I agree," said Nina. "I couldn't think of a better man for the job than Barbara."

Fuzzy looked back and forth from Nina to Max, trying to decode what must be a joke. He had thought he was starting to understand human jokes, but now he was not so sure.

"I hate to tell you this, Fuzzy," said Nina. "But you're out of a job. They sent Barbara instead. They said she had the sort of primal instincts and seriously butt-kicking fuzzy logic needed to pull off the mission. And, well . . . you didn't. You hesitated, when your own existence was at stake, to take the necessary action. And Barbara didn't."

"What do you mean 'sent' her? Sent her where?"

"To Mars!" yelled Max.

"You see, Fuzzy," said Nina, "Jones and his team put your body back together again . . . but stuck on the backup head . . . with Barbara's code in it."

Fuzzy didn't say anything.

"Don't you get it, Fuzz? They stuck *her* in the rocket and blasted *her* off to Mars! She's long gone! She went on the mission instead of you."

Fuzzy sat there for a long time.

"Frozen up?" asked Max.

"No," said Fuzzy. "Just not sure what to do next."

"Well," said Nina. "Right now, we've got your head running on an older body, but it's not bad. Not good enough for Mars, but good enough for here. Now that we don't have to send you off to Mars, the Robot Integration Program is finally *really* about robot integration. Jones and Ryder are off overseeing the Mars mission, and

I'm in charge. Jones was right, you did make a lot of progress—even if he got a little overexcited about it. But it was only for a couple of weeks. I want to see what happens when you stay in school for a couple of years."

"She means that you're staying here," said Max. "In school. With me!"

Fuzzy sat quietly for a few seconds, then stood up.

"In that case," said Fuzzy, "aren't we late for Mr. Xu's class?"

"Oh smoke, I forgot. C'mon, Fuzzy!"

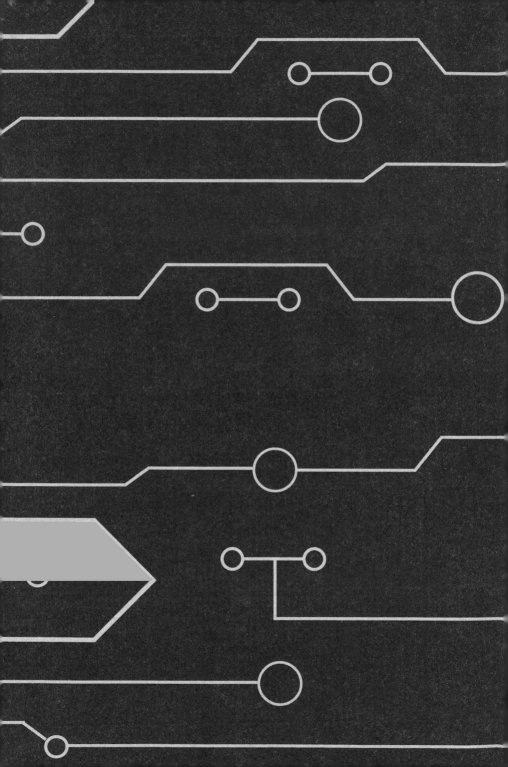

TOM ANGLEBERGER is the author of the bestselling Origami Yoda series, as well as *Horton Halfpott* and *Fake Mustache*, both Edgar Award nominees, the Qwikpick Papers series, and the Inspector Flytrap series. He lives in Christiansburg, Virginia, with his wife, the author/illustrator Cece Bell. Visit Tom online at www.origamiyoda.com.

PAUL DELLINGER is a former newspaper reporter who writes science fiction and fantasy stories, many of which are collected in the book *Mr. Lazarus and Other Stories*.